WINTER'S KISS

DEE DAVIS

Published by Pocito Press.

Cover design: Rogenna Brewer

ISBN: 978-0-9971834-5-0

http://www.deedavis.com

ACKNOWLEDGMENTS

Acknowledgements:

Writing novels is a solitary occupation, but publishing them requires a team. I'd like to thank mine. To my bestie Julie Kenner who always helps to make my work stronger. To my mother who finds the most hilarious mistakes and always makes me laugh. And to my editors Melody Brislin and Kim Huther who keep me on the straight and narrow. And finally to my readers—none of this would be possible without you!

CHAPTER 1

Scottish Highlands – 1467

When Ailis Davidson dreamt of Tur nan Clach it wasn't of dark, dirty cages or cold, dank dungeons. It wasn't of her brother's angry threats or cruel punishments. It was of sun-kissed stone and purple fields of heather. It was the dark green of the trees and the blue-black of the craggy mountains. The smell of peat fires and loamy earth. The sound of water rushing in the burn and the lonely cry of the kestrel.

The trees overhead rattled, the cold wind shaking winter-bare branches, pulling her from her thoughts. The path here was barely more than a trail, rutted and worn. What was left of the sun slipped in the sky as her party made its way deeper into the forest. Despite her escort, it had been a lonely journey, but there was nothing new in that.

As much as she had loved her time at Duncreag, and tolerated her time at Moy, her most fervent wish had always been to come home. And until now, it had seemed impossible. Although her brother was dead, his men scattered to the winds, Tur nan Clach had been out of reach. A dream she'd never hoped to see coming to fruition.

But now Uncle Lyall was dead. Which made her the surviving Davidson. And as such, she alone was responsible for her clan. She tightened her hands on the reins of her mount, the gray mare tossing her head as if she, too, scented the smells of home.

Bound by the Chief of Chattan at Moy, Ailis had feared at first that the laird would forbid her journey. He had argued that she needed a husband. A man to protect and defend her right to her holding. But Ailis had stood strong, fighting his wishes. In all truth, she had had enough of men and their posturing.

Well, maybe not all men. Her lips tipped in a smile, but she pushed the thought away.

Ranald Macqueen was not interested in settling down with anyone. And neither was she. Their lives were on different paths. Her future lay at Tur nan Clach. And his? Well, wherever he was, she was certain he was not thinking of her. Not after everything her brother had done.

Ailis pulled her cloak closer, shifting on her mare as she watched the evening mist shrouding the ground and twisting through the trees.

"Are ye calt then, my lady?" Jeane Slorach asked, the maidservant's tone belying any real concern.

"Nay, 'tis only the deepening shadows." Ailis pushed the past from her mind, squaring her shoulders and lifting her chin. Clan Davidson was her heritage. The fact that she was a woman should have no bearing.

Except that, of course, it did. Ailis shivered again as she considered the enormity of what she sought to achieve.

"I canna say that I ken why you chose to leave Moy for the likes o' this." Jeane waved a hand at the rough countryside surrounding the road, her craggy face settling into lines of resentment.

Her maid had been the first to object to traveling to Tur nan Clach—the ends of the earth as she'd put it. Not that Ailis could blame her.

Tur nan Clach was far from any semblance of civilization. If Ailis were honest, that's why she loved it. Somewhere far away from all the machinations that made up the court at Moy. Of course, simply coming home could not erase her brother's sins. She blew out a long breath, guilt washing through her even as old injuries resurfaced.

The important point was that she'd survived and that she wasn't Alisdair. While living at Duncreag, she'd realized that life could be made up of more than blind ambition and cruel threats. Watching Katherine and Iain, she'd witnessed true love. Something she'd seen little enough of in her short life.

She shivered again and glanced ahead at the two Chattan men who rode in front, trees arching over them like silent sentries. Andro Mackay's head was bent as he whispered something to his companion after shooting a narrowed-eyed glance over his shoulder. The man had made it more than clear that he suffered his duty only by direct order of his laird. He had no real fealty to her or her clan. Nor did the others.

Four escorts and Jeane. And not even her maid held any allegiance. She, too, had been forced into the job, Ailis's potentially rash decision impacting all of their lives. For a moment, she felt another twinge of guilt, but she forced the feeling away.

Her companions may not have chosen this journey, but they owed their loyalty to Duncan Macintosh. And the Laird of Chattan had ordered their obedience. He might believe she would fail, but ultimately he hadn't tried to stop her when she'd insisted on going. And despite the veiled

3

animosity of those traveling with her, she wasn't fool enough to begrudge their protection.

There were those who would relish seeing her fail.

As if to underscore the point, her horse shied and snorted as a shadow separated itself from the gloom of the sheltering trees. Then, with cries like banshees, men on horses crashed from the winter-bare vegetation in front of them, claymores raised as they charged.

Metal clashed against metal as Andro and his men entered the fray. Jeane screamed and Ailis drew her dirk, wishing she had a better weapon. The tiny knife was not meant to hold sway against men with swords.

Her protectors surged forward. In a panic Jeane kneed her horse, and instead of pulling away from danger, charged directly into it. Ailis cried out, but it was too late; one of their attackers sliced through the maid with his claymore. Bile flooded Ailis's throat as Jeane fell to the ground, her lifeless body trampled beneath the hooves of the fighting men.

A large man separated himself from the fight, his dark eyes locking with hers as he rode toward her, his sword arm raised high. Fear lanced through her as she tried to turn her horse. But the mare was panicked, rearing up to paw the air, eyes wild, the animal's heated breath forming white mist in the cold air.

The man moved closer, bloodlust shining in his eyes. Ailis yanked the reins, trying for control, but the mare would have none of it; instead, seeming determined to escape the melee sans rider. With a powerful leap, the horse sent Ailis flying. She slammed into the ground at the foot of a rowan tree, the low-hanging branches momentarily thwarting her attacker's approach.

Fighting a wave of dizziness, she struggled to her feet, ignoring the pain as she sprinted deeper into the cover of the forest. She could hear the man and his horse crashing through the brush behind her. Fear clawed at her, compelling her to run harder—branches slapping at her face as thorns tore her garments and scratched her arms.

The mist was rising, swirling now as high as her shoulders, darkness descending as the sun was swallowed by the mountains. The shadows were her friends, cloaking her from her enemy, but she knew he was still out there. Listening. Hunting. Waiting for her to make a mistake. Ahead, a darker shadow loomed from the mist. Something solid. Man-made.

Sucking in a ragged breath, she rushed through a gap in a pile of fallen stone. Beyond that the skeleton of a building rose out of the gloom, and she instantly recognized where she was. Cuimeanach Abbey. Or what was left of it. The derelict chapel had long been abandoned, the roof gaping open to the stars, the arched windows hollow and empty.

Somewhere off to her left she heard the sounds of the horseman, still in pursuit. No doubt others would be joining him. She could continue to run, but sooner or later they'd find her. Better to seek shelter. Pray that she could find somewhere safe to hide.

Using trees for cover, she made her way across the small clearing to the abbey's front door. The massive slab of oak hung from one broken hinge, the carved relief completely worn away in places. Slipping through the narrow opening, she risked waiting a moment for her eyes to adjust to the dark interior.

Cold and musty, the arched room was open to the sky in places, fallen stone littering the floor of what had once been a magnificent chapel. Something moved in the corner, rocks skittering against the flagged floor. Ailis shivered, pulling her cloak closer as she moved farther inside. At the far end of the cavernous room stood the remains of an altar, the marble structure broken and slanted upward toward the ceiling. Just beyond the altar, through a crumbling archway, she could make out the shadowy shapes of stone effigies.

A crypt.

Behind her, a horse's hooves clattered against the cobblestoned courtyard. Heart racing, she dashed past the altar and through the archway. The crypt was shrouded in shadows, but Ailis could make out the carved visages of a knight and his lady. People who'd long ago lived and loved—and died.

A shudder of fear slid down her spine as she pressed herself into a narrow crevice between the effigies and the wall. She hadn't had the chance to live, let alone love. Yet death surrounded her, and as she heard the sound of leather against stone, she shrank deeper into the shadows, trying to disappear.

Outside in the chapel she could hear movement, and then a whoosh of air followed by a crash as something fell to the floor and shattered. Cringing, she pressed closer into the tiny space, her back to the wall, her face pressed against the base of the knight's tomb. Cold curled through her like icy fingers, and her heart pounded against her chest. The footsteps grew closer, the scrape of the man's sword as he searched the crypt's crevices and corners echoing in the stillness.

She even fancied she could hear him breathe. She wasn't sure what she feared most. Death, or what might befall her if the warrior didn't kill her. Despite years of torment at her brother's hands she had remained a maiden, and the thought of being defiled in such a way sent a fresh wave of terror rocking through her.

Boot heels echoed against the stone floor just on the other side of the tombs. She pressed closer to the knight, praying that he would somehow rise and protect her. Madness surely, but she had nothing left. Her hand moved frantically over the floor beneath her, searching for a weapon. She'd lost her dirk when the mare had thrown her.

"I know yer in here, ye brazen witch." The man's voice was little more than a snarl. "It's no use runnin', yer companions are dead."

Even though she'd barely known them, she felt a rush of anger and guilt, the image of Jeane's trampled body racing through her mind. All of this was her fault. If she hadn't been so headstrong. If she hadn't wanted so very much to do right by the people of Tur nan Clach.

Her blood stilled, her skin prickling with renewed fear.

There was no escaping the fact that the holding, though small, was valuable. And clearly someone wanted to take it from her. Or better yet, eliminate the threat she posed.

"Ye ken that I'll no' leave until I've found you," the man called, his voice closer now, his tone menacing. "I canna return without proof that yer dead..." The voice trailed off, his footsteps moving closer to the crevice where she was hiding.

Ailis tried to swallow the fear rising in her throat as she pressed closer to the base of the tomb. There was no way out. Nothing she could do but stay hidden and pray.

As if God had time for someone like her.

The man suddenly loomed above her, his claymore raised as his lips twisted. "I've got ye now," he snarled. "And I intend to make you pay fer that dash through the woods."

He reached down and grabbed her wrist, yanking her from the crevice, her cloak tearing away as her bodice caught on the tip of the entombed knight's stone sword. She struggled to free herself, but her attacker's grip was bruising as he slammed her back against the wall, his rank body pressing tight against hers. She choked on bile, fear combining with disgust as he used his other hand to grab at her breast.

After everything she'd lived through, it seemed unfair

that this was to be the end. He forced her head back, trying to kiss her, but she turned her head. In anger, he twisted her arm until her wrist felt like it would break. Still she continued to fight, using elbows and feet, but he was too big and his hold on her too tight.

"Yer a comely lass with a fighting spirit." His lips parted in a feral smile, his blackened teeth making her stomach churn. "I'll enjoy taking ye before ye die." His grin widened as he stroked her skin.

She opened her mouth to scream but his lips covered hers, his tongue forcing its way inside. His stench made her gut heave. Terror clawed at her, and she bit him. Hard.

"Sodding whore," the man roared as he reared back, slamming his fist into her cheek.

Her head cracked against the stone wall and the world went white, then black—everything spinning, pain crashing through her head. As she struggled to regain her footing her attacker tightened his hold, pushing a knee between her legs as he fumbled with his other hand to raise her skirts.

"No, please. I—" Ailis hated the note of pleading in her voice but it was as if she had no choice, the words springing fresh from her fear. Sucking in a breath, she forced herself to still, her eyes fixing on the wall just beyond the knight's effigy. If nothing else, she'd hold on to her dignity. It was all she had left.

The man's fingers dug into her shoulder, his rancid breath hot against her cheek as he crushed his mouth against hers. Ailis swallowed a scream, knowing that there was no one to hear. She was alone. Always alone.

Struggling to breathe as he continued to grope and paw, she started to close her eyes. Behind him the air seemed to shimmer, as if a gauzy curtain had descended. Then, suddenly, a woman sprang from nowhere, appearing it seemed from thin air on the other side of the tomb. The

8

lady's eyes widened in shock and then quickly narrowed, flashing with anger as she recognized the man's intent.

"What the hell do you think you're doing?" she barked, striding forward like a man, waving a large metal shovel, the end looking wickedly pointed and sharp. "Let her go, you son of a bitch." The cadence of her speech made her words hard to understand, but Ailis gratefully followed the gist. And so did the swine who held her.

"What's this then," he growled, spinning to face the new threat. "Two fer the price o' one?"

Without hesitation, the woman lifted the shovel and swung it with all her might. Caught by surprise, the man's expression was almost comical as the shovel connected with his head; the satisfying thwack of metal against bone more pleasing than Ailis was willing to admit.

With a groan her attacker fell to the floor, his sword clattering against the stone.

For a moment both women stared at the fallen man, then Ailis took a faltering step forward. "Is he…is he dead?"

No." The other woman shook her head. "Although he damn well deserves to be. He's just out cold. Are you all right?"

"I think so," Ailis said, her head still spinning as she pulled her tattered gown together to cover her breasts.

"But you're bleeding." The woman frowned.

Ailis raised a hand to her head, her fingers coming away sticky with blood. Her stomach revolted at the sight, and she struggled to keep from casting her accounts. "'Tis nothing." She waved a hand but the movement sent pain cascading through her, and she stumbled against the knight's effigy.

"He hit you pretty hard," the woman said, her expression colored with concern.

Ailis released a shaky sigh, her legs wobbling as she kept a hand on the tomb for support. "He was going to do a great deal more. But thanks to you, he did not."

"Thanks to me, he'll have a hell of headache when he wakes." The woman shot a look at the prostrate man. "Hopefully not any time soon."

"Still," Ailis said, wiping blood from her eyes, "there could be more of them. We need to go."

"No." The woman shook her head. "*You* have to go."

Ailis swayed again fighting the pain. "But I canna leave you here—with him."

"I'll be fine here. I'll just go back where I came from."

A shiver worked its way up Ailis's spine, the memory of the woman's shimmery arrival playing through her head. She'd prayed for a miracle, but now she wasn't quite sure what to do with it. "Who are you?" she whispered, her hands shaking now from more than pain.

"Quinn." The woman smiled, the affectation making her look younger. Not much older than Ailis.

Ailis repeated the name with a nod. No matter where Quinn had come from, it was clear that she was a friend. And without her help…

"But how is it you're here at all?" Ailis forced out the words, as Quinn kicked away the man's sword. "It seemed to me as if you appeared from…nowhere."

"I'm not sure that I can adequately explain it." Quinn shrugged, her fist clenching nervously. "And even if I could, I'm not sure you'd believe me."

"Are you fey then?" The words came of their own accord, and Ailis immediately felt foolish.

Quinn's laughter filled the crypt. "Hardly. I'm as human as you. I'm an archeologist."

The word had no meaning, but Ailis nodded as if it made sense.

"I was working here in the abbey and I found something."

She opened her fisted hand to reveal a finely-wrought clan badge. It glinted silver in the pale light, its only flaw a small notch in one side. The word *courage* was carved across the top. "When I touch it...hold it..." Quinn trailed off with a frown.

Clarity dawned as Ailis thought of Iain's Katherine. "You travel through time."

Surprise crested on Quinn's face, but she nodded as she looked down at the image of a rampant lion she held in her hand. "I wouldn't have thought...at least I'd have expected you to be more—" She stopped, clearly embarrassed.

"Frightened?" Despite the pounding pain, Ailis felt her mouth twitch with a smile. "I suppose I should be. But without you, I'd be..." She waved a hand at her attacker's prone form. "What do I care how you came to be here?"

"Yes, but you don't even seem surprised, really."

Ailis shrugged with a casualness she did not feel. "I canna explain fully, but though a rare magic, 'tis true that I believe such things are possible." She thought of Katherine and the wonders she'd described. "Do you come from Connecticut?" The word still sounded strange as she struggled to pronounce it.

Quinn's eyebrows rose again. "No. I'm from Texas, actually. But I'm here now. In Scotland, I mean. Working in the abbey. Only, in my time." She frowned. "It's all so confusing. I found the brooch here." She pointed to the edge the tombs, by the lady's stone feet. "And when I touched it..." She lifted her troubled gaze to meet Ailis's.

"You traveled to my time."

Quinn nodded.

"Have you done this before?" Ailis asked, reaching for the effigy again as another wave of dizziness washed through her.

"Only a few times," Quinn confessed. "The first by accident. The second just to prove I'd done it." She frowned. "And then today, I don't know, I felt compelled somehow. And it-turns out I was right."

"You saved my life."

"Well, perhaps one day you can return the favor," Quinn replied with a soft smile. "But not unless you make your escape now." She glanced first at the fallen man and then out into the chapel. "You need to go."

"Aye." Ailis nodded, reality slamming back into place, the magic of the moment gone. She pushed blood-soaked hair from her face and sucked in a breath, her cheek throbbing as she gathered her strength. "You're certain you won't come with me?"

"Honestly, there's no need," Quinn said as they made their way to the broken doorway. "And besides, I'm not quite sure what would happen if I left here. Up until now it's just been me. And I've only stayed a moment. This is the first time I've encountered anyone else. Here, like this, I mean. For all I know, I've already upset some cosmic plan."

"Well, if you have, I thank God for it."

"Still, it's better for you to go. And once I'm sure you're safely away, I'll go back. Or forward." She frowned then lifted her hands. "Or whatever."

They stopped just outside the chapel doorway, the attacker's horse stamping impatiently against the cobbled courtyard. Ailis reached for the woman's hand, her fingers closing over the palm holding the clan badge. Heat streaked up her arm, the impact jarring, and she jerked free. "'Tis indeed powerful magic, whatever it is. I wish you well."

"And I you." Quinn stepped back, gesturing toward the abbey's gate. "Now go."

Ailis nodded and then turned, her mind spinning as she struggled through her pain to make sense of all that had happened. She reached for the reins then stopped and turned back, half expecting Quinn to have already disappeared. But instead the other woman was standing just outside the door —the badge in one hand, the strange shovel held firmly in the other.

"My name is Ailis," she called, compelled to offer Quinn something, if only her name. "Ailis Davidson. If you should ever find yourself in need, go to Duncreag. It's just north of the River Findhorn. They'll understand. And they'll know where to find me."

"Thank you, Ailis." Quinn gave a sharp nod. "But I'll be fine. It's you I'm concerned about. Are you sure you can manage?" She glanced up at the restless horse.

"It doesn't really matter. In truth, I have no choice."

"You're right." She looked like she wanted to say more, but instead she tilted her chin toward the horse. "Go quickly. Before the asshole wakes up. And Ailis, be careful."

Ailis smiled at the odd, but apt, moniker. "You, as well." She lifted a hand and then, fighting against the pain, swung into the saddle, praying that her new friend would indeed be safe. With a sigh, she turned the horse to the north. Toward safety. Toward Duncreag.

And when she looked back into the shadowed courtyard —it was empty.

Quinn was gone.

CHAPTER 2

"God's blood, whose idea was it to come to this forsaken part of the Highlands in the first place?"

Ranald Macqueen grinned at his eldest brother, Kendric, as he urged his horse forward, adjusting his cloak while the thick, icy mist twirled around them. "As I recall, brother o' mine, 'twas your idea."

The deepening shadows stretched across the narrow track they'd been following for the last couple of days. Their cousin Iain Mackintosh's holding was located in rustic country on the edge of the Cairngorm Mountains.

"Aye, that it was," Benneit, Ranald's other brother, his father's proverbial spare, replied, his eyes on Kendric. "You're the one who was sore in need of escaping our mother's matrimonial manipulations."

"Dinna think you can escape her conniving just because you're a wee bit younger," Kendric groused. "I've no doubt she's just waiting to find the right lass for each of us. Given her head, she'd have us all leg-shackled in no time at all."

"Aye, but as long as you remain a free man—Ranald and I are safe from her evil eye."

Ranald laughed at the idea of anyone referring to his diminutive mother's bright blue eyes as evil. Even with three strapping grown-up sons, Ealasaid Macqueen was still a slip of a woman with the power to take away a man's ability to breathe. The only possible fault she could be accused of was the overwhelming desire to see her sons well and truly settled—long before any of them were ready to give up their wandering ways.

"As long as there are comely lasses willing to open their legs without the promise of marriage," Kendric opined, "I see no point in needlessly tying myself to only one woman. No matter what my darlin' mother might have to say on the subject."

"Yet, your inability to stand up and tell her exactly that, is why we're here in the middle of nowhere on a journey to escape, as you so succinctly put it, a fate worse than death."

"I'm no' saying I never want to marry. Just not now. And not Elena Macswan."

"You could do far worse," Ranald suggested. The Macswan lass was comely enough. Although a bit quick of temper. All that red hair no doubt.

"I mean no disrespect to the lass," Kendric said. "She just is no' the one for me."

"Have you someone in mind then?" Benneit asked.

"Nay. But I'll know her when I see her." Kendric urged his horse around a fallen tree, the mist almost making it invisible in the deepening gloom.

"You sound like Iain." Ranald followed his brother around the obstruction, bare tree branches pulling at his cloak.

"Mayhap I do," Kendric said, "but you canna say that turned out fer naught."

Ranald had to admit that Iain had found his true mate in Katherine St. Claire. Theirs was a rare kind of love. The same as his parents shared. Most men weren't lucky enough to find the perfect mate—their other half. If Ranald should ever find a woman like that, well, then he might just be willing to consider trading his freedom. But of course he wasn't about to admit any of that to his brothers. Being the youngest, they already gave him enough grief. And besides, he was more than happy with his life just the way it was.

For a moment he had a vision of crystal blue eyes and hair soft as silk, the color of moonlight. He shook his head, banishing the thought. There was nothing served in wishing for what could never be his. Truth be told, he wasn't even sure he wanted it.

"Cat got your tongue then, brother?" Benneit pressed, a hint of laughter underscoring his words. "Never figured you'd be one to moon over a woman."

For a moment Ranald had the horrifying thought that his brother had read his mind, but then at Kendric's raised eyebrows he realized that they were speaking of the tavern wench at the inn where they'd stopped for food and ale. The lass had been more than clear about what she was willing to offer. But to make Duncreag by nightfall there hadn't been time to tarry.

As it was, the heavy mist had slowed them considerably, darkness now fully upon them.

"She was a comely lass, but I'm no' sorry to have moved on. Truth be told, there'll always be another one."

"And therein lies our brother's conundrum. Please our mother and lose out on all those bonnie lasses or continue to philander and risk her ire."

"Hence heading for the hills." Kendric grinned.

"Literally," Ranald groused as his horse momentarily lost its footing on the scree. They rounded a bend to the sound of rushing water. "'Tis the river. No' much farther now." In the distance, high on a rocky crag, faint light glittered through the trees. "Look up there," he pointed. "You can just make out the walls o' Duncreag."

A sudden, sharp longing shot through him. As much as he cared about home, he also loved the fierce beauty of this country. He'd spent almost as much time here as he had at Corybrough. First when he and Iain were younger, and then serving for a short time as his cousin's captain, although Fergus Mackintosh still officially held the title. The old man was unwilling to cede his authority—even to Ranald.

In the end, it had been easier to answer his father's call and head home to fight with his brothers against a rival clan. Unfortunately, battle won, his mother had settled into other ideas. And so his brothers had readily volunteered to accompany him when he'd professed the need to return to Duncreag.

Hopefully, his cousin would be glad to see him. When he'd left, Katherine was just beginning her confinement. The babe would be near to coming if he reckoned right. A prick of something he wasn't ready to acknowledge washed through him at the thought of his cousin becoming a father. Not that he begrudged Iain his happiness.

"Are you going to sit and stare until our ballocks freeze off?" Kendric taunted, pulling Ranald from his rambling thoughts. "Or will you ride with us to the tower?"

"Give it a rest, you bleedin' arse." He spurred his horse onward, anxious for the warmth and welcome waiting at Duncreag.

As they made their way across a shallow ford in the river the clouds broke for a moment, moonlight glittering on the water. The night was still, the quiet almost deafening. Ranald felt a pricking across the back of his neck and shot a look of warning at his brothers.

Kendric nodded, his hand moving to the strap of the scabbard across his back. Benneit, too, reached for his weapon, deftly drawing his sword. Ranald swept his gaze slowly across the line of trees as they moved out of the river onto the stone-studded bank.

A gust of wind blew through the branches, whistling eerily as it moved through the twirling mist. The moon disappeared again amidst the clouds, the dark seeming menacing now. They moved forward slowly, Ranald not certain why he felt wary, but equally positive that there was a reason.

The bushes ahead rattled ominously, the mist scattering in the wake of something crashing out of the underbrush. Ranald drew his claymore, tensing for battle as a horse leapt out of the trees, its eyes wild with fright as it reared, hooves pawing the night.

"Hold," Kendric said, lifting a hand in the air. "There's no rider."

"Does no' mean 'tis no' a threat," Benneit warned as the beast dropped to its feet again, flanks heaving as it eyed the other horses.

Ranald sheathed his sword and circled slowly round the horse, his brothers still with their claymores at the ready. Reaching down he grabbed the reins, speaking in soft nonsensical words in an attempt to ease the beast's fear.

"There's nothing here to mark ownership," Ranald said with a frown as he leaned over to stroke the horse's nose, his own mount remaining firmly under control.

"There must be a rider nearby." Benneit moved toward the edge of the trees where the frantic horse had emerged. The wind gusted again, this time on a long, low moan. The stillness that followed was broken by a softer, quieter groan.

"That sounds human." Kendric edged closer to the trees.

"If someone is hurt we should offer aid," Benneit said.

"Aye, but it could also be a trap." Kendric frowned as the sound emanated from the undergrowth again.

"To hell with your bletherin'." Ranald slid off of his mount, and headed into the bushes, sword at the ready. "You're no better than a pair o'wee bairns."

"I reckon we'd best follow him," Kendric grumbled as he dropped from his horse to follow Ranald, Benneit right behind. "Mother would ne'er forgive us if anything happened to the little bastard."

Ignoring his brothers, Ranald moved slowly into the woods. The mist swirled almost to his waist and, between it and the gnarled tree branches, it was hard to see anything but shifting shadows. Off to his left the soft, hollow sound of a moan filled the dark space.

"Over here," he called to his brothers as he moved forward, dirk drawn.

A flash of something pale against the pine needles and dead leaves that covered the forest floor snagged his attention and he quickly covered the distance. Silvery hair fanned out across the frozen ground, fair skin gleaming in the filtered moonlight.

A woman.

Sheathing his weapon, he knelt beside her, careful not to jar her with his movements. His brothers broke into the little clearing, stumbling to a halt, Benneit crossing himself. "Is she still alive?"

Sliding fingers across the smooth column of her throat, he felt the flutter of her life's blood and released a breath he hadn't realized he'd been holding. "Aye, barely." Slowly, trying not to jostle her more than necessary, he rolled her over to her back, her moan making him stop, the faint light striking her face.

"Ailis." His heart stuttered and he felt as if he'd been punched in the gullet.

"Ye know her?" Kendric asked in astonishment.

"I do." He brushed the hair back from her bloodstained face. "She's Alisdair Davidson's sister."

"The man who tried to kill Iain's Katherine?" Benneit queried, anger coloring his voice.

"Aye, but Ailis had no part in that. In fact, she as much as anyone suffered at her brother's hands." Just the thought of the hell Alisdair had put his sister through made his blood boil. "She is a friend to both Iain and Katherine. And I'll no' have you thinking otherwise."

"Easy, brother," Kendric said. "We've naught against the girl. Although if we dinna get her warm soon, what we think of her won't have any relevance at all."

Shaking his head at his own ineptitude, Ranald carefully slid his arms beneath Ailis' slender frame. She moaned and her eyelashes fluttered, opening to reveal the deep blue of her eyes. For a moment she frowned, and then her lips lifted in the tiniest of smiles. "Ranald," she whispered.

"Hush now," he crooned as he swung her up into his arms and made his way back to the horses. "You're safe now."

She watched him for a moment and then nodded, curling into his chest. "Two miracles," she said on a sigh as she lapsed back into sleep.

"Give her to me," Kendric said, already mounted.

"Nay," Ranald said, passing Ailis to Benneit and swinging up onto his horse. "I'll carry her."

Kendric eyed his brother for a moment, as if to argue, but then nodded. "Fine then. But let us hurry."

Benneit handed Ailis to Ranald, and he wrapped his cloak around her as he cradled her against his body. Her breathing was shallow, and even with the impatient movements of the horse she didn't stir. Fear gouged deep into his belly and he held her closer as they moved along the path, Duncreag still visible amongst the trees in the fading moonlight.

His heart twisted as he glanced down at her still, pale

features. Even in repose she was beautiful. Anger rose, hot and heavy, and he swore on everything he held holy that whoever had done this to her would pay.

～

"What news?" Ranald asked as Iain Macintosh walked toward him across the great hall. His breath caught at the somber expression on his cousin's face. "Is she…"

"Nay." Iain shook his head, settling into a large chair near the fire. "But she still sleeps. Katherine says it will help her to heal, but the blow to her head was a fierce one."

"Not to mention the exposure to the wet and cold," Benneit said as he poured Iain a tankard of ale. "I'd no' give odds that a grown man could withstand all o' that. Let alone a wee lass."

"She's going to be fine," Ranald ground out. "Katherine is well versed in the healing arts. She'll find a way to make her well."

"Mayhap, but there are limits even to Katherine's magic." Kendric laid a hand briefly on Ranald's shoulder, the touch meant to comfort. But Ranald shook it off, moving to pace in front of the stone fireplace.

"Ailis is a fighter. She'll no' give up."

"Aye, she is that," Iain agreed. "And with Katherine's aid hopefully she'll wake soon, but until then there is naught for us to do but wait."

"Something Ranald has never been good at," Benneit offered.

"It's just that I feel responsible. If we'd not tarried at the inn, we'd have come across her horse sooner. Had her here and warm that much faster."

"Or we'd have missed her altogether," Kendric said.

"There's no use second-guessing what might have been. Best to concentrate on the here and now."

"And to that end," Iain said, sipping his ale, "did you see signs of anyone else? The attacker or others who might have been traveling with her?"

"Nay," Ranald replied. "There was no sign of others. But there was no time for a thorough search. Benneit did have a quick look, though."

"I found no signs of anyone beyond Ailis and her horse. Does she live near enough that she'd have been out on her own?"

Iain shook his head. "Since her uncle was given the laird-ship of Tur nan Clach, she's been living at Moy. Under Uncle Duncan's protection."

"I thought she'd inherited the holding." Ranald frowned, remembering Ailis' desire to right the many wrongs her brother had inflicted on his people.

"By blood rights, she did," Iain replied. "But she is a woman. And Lyall made a convincing plea as to his capabilities to serve as laird in her stead."

"And did he prove a capable leader?" Kendric asked.

"Depends on how you define the word," Iain spat. "I've no admiration for the man. Like Alisdair, he held control by threats and fear."

"Held?" Ranald tilted his head, considering the implications behind the word.

"Aye. Lyall Davidson is dead. The story is that he was killed in a skirmish with a band of reivers."

"But you dinna believe it to be so?" Kendric poured himself more ale.

"I've no idea where the truth lies. But the livestock at Tur nan Clach is scrawny at best. What there is of it."

"You believe there was something else behind the attack."

"I canna say for certain. But, yes, it seems to me there is more afoot."

"And regardless of the why of it, the uncle is dead," Benneit said, his gaze speculative. "And Tur nan Clach is again without a laird."

"Which could explain why Ailis was out there," Iain offered.

"Aye," Ranald agreed. "If her uncle was as bad as you say, she'd still be wanting to put things to rights."

Ailis had made it clear the last time they'd been together, nothing was more important to her than Tur nan Clach. The needs of her people would always come first. They alone held her heart. Which, at the time, had suited him just fine.

"But surely she would no' have been traveling on her own," Benneit surmised, eyes narrowing as he leaned forward, resting his elbows on his knees.

"I canna imagine your uncle would have allowed her to leave on her own."

"Aye, but as we've said, there was no sign of anyone else. And Ailis is no' a fool." Ranald knew there had to be more to the story. Ailis was a strong woman, despite her tiny stature, and she was also a smart one. She'd not be traveling on her own unless there was a good reason.

"Did Katherine find…" Kendric trialed off, his face turning red. "I mean to say, was she violated in any way?"

Ranald's stomach clenched. There was a moment of silence and then Iain shook his head. "Katherine says no. But in light of the evidence 'tis possible she was attacked with that intent. Her overdress was torn, as was her chemise. And there are bruises on her mouth and neck, as well as scratches on her thighs and breasts."

Ranald fisted a hand, bringing it down hard upon the arm of his chair. "The whoreson."

"Easy, little brother," Benneit said. "Wait until we have a

culprit to punish. That chair has done naught to offend you."

"I canna countenance a man who needs to force a woman," Ranald growled, his mind's eye presenting an image of a dimpled cheek and sunny smile. Ailis deserved so much more than this.

"Nor I," Kendric agreed. "But Benneit is right; there's naught to be done until we know who it was that attacked the girl."

"And unfortunately, 'tis possible we'll ne'er know the answer to that." Benneit sounded almost apologetic.

"I'll have my men ride to the site at first light. Kendric, you'll guide them?" Iain asked.

"Nay," Ranald spoke, the word sounding harsh. "I'll go."

"'Tis better if you stay here," Kendric offered. "When she awakens, she'll need a friend. And 'twas you who found her."

There was merit in what his brother said. But the idea of doing nothing did not sit well.

"Kendric is right," Iain said. "Ailis has always been fond of you. 'Twould do her good to know that you're here. And once we know what we're dealing with, then you can take action."

"I agree with Iain," Katherine interjected, her hands resting protectively across her swollen belly as she walked across the great hall to sit beside her husband. "Ailis will want to see you when she wakes."

"But she has you and Iain. She has no need of me." Even as he protested, he felt the desire to see her. To hold her hands and wait for her eyes to open, to light with recognition.

Katherine's knowing gaze collided with his. "It is different and you know it. You found her and brought her to us. She'll want you near."

"You canna know that," Ranald continued to argue.

"Oh, but I can." Katherine's smile widened. "For it is your name she calls as she fights to live."

CHAPTER 3

*T*he world was shrouded in shadow, deep and dark, pulling at her with clammy fingers. Ailis could feel cold stone against her back. She struggled to move, but her limbs refused the order. Panic rose, black and thick, twining around her heart and lungs. She tried to breathe through the fear, but suddenly a face loomed in darkness.

The man in the crypt. He was alive. His hands dug into her shoulders and she swallowed a scream, determined to fight, but she still couldn't move. His lips parted, his feral snarl frightening with its salacious intent. He moved closer, so close she could feel his putrid breath. She moaned, twisting her head. Praying for release.

The face drew even nearer, shifting in the shadows. Not her attacker. Alisdair. Her brother was here. She tried to break free of his punishing hold, but he laughed with a sneer.

"Did you think to escape me, little sister? To break free from that which you owe me?"

She shook her head, shrinking back against the sharp stones, ignoring the pain, trying only to free herself from the nightmare that ensnared her.

Alisdair was dead and buried. Gone. He could never hurt her again.

His fingers dug into the skin beneath her chin as he forced her to look him in the eyes. "You will always belong to me, Ailis. You're nothing in your own right. Merely a possession to do with as I please."

"No," she begged, hating herself for giving into the fear. But Alisdair knew how to punish her. How to play upon the things that terrified her. Places dark and cold and ugly. She shivered, and tried again to pull free. "You're dead," she whispered. "Dead."

"Ailis." The man's voice rumbled through her, touching something deep inside. "You're safe. No one can hurt you." Alisdair's face faded as callused fingers gently brushed the hair from her forehead. "'Tis all right, lass. I'm here. I'll no' let anyone hurt you."

The sound of his voice soothed her as much as his words, pulling her from the horrible darkness. Away from the shadows. Away from her brother's wrath. Her eyes flickered opened. "Ranald." She breathed the name as if it were a prayer.

And perhaps it was.

"There now," he said, his dark eyes filled with concern. "There's nothing more to fear. You're safe here. Nothing can harm you."

"Where...where am I?" she asked, eyes moving around the dimly lit chamber.

"Duncreag," he answered. "My brothers and I found you in the woods and brought you here."

She struggled to remember. The attack in the forest, the man in the crypt.

Quinn.

"There was a woman. She helped me."

"You were alone when we found you." Ranald frowned, and absurdly she wanted to soothe away his worry.

She swallowed, but the words wouldn't come.

She was so tired. And yet she was afraid to close her eyes. Afraid of what the dark might yet hold. Perhaps the darkness was the reality and this the dream.

"All is well, Ailis," Ranald assured her, reaching out to stroke her hair. "I swear it." He sat beside her on the bed. "You're among friends, now. And we will no' let anything more happen to you."

She nodded, licking dry lips. He sat beside her on the bed, sliding a strong arm beneath her shoulders. "Here, drink this." He lifted a cup and helped her take a sip. The ale was cool, the taste sharp against her tongue.

He lay her back against the pillows and she sighed, missing his touch as he moved to stand. "I'll just go and get Katherine. She'll be so relieved to know that you're awake."

Panic licked at the edges of consciousness. "No." Her voice cracked as she reached for his hand. "I do not want to be alone. Stay with me until I sleep?" She hated the pleading in her voice. Hated that she needed him. Needed anyone, really. But she couldn't seem to stop herself. "Please."

His expression softened as he sat beside her again, his strong fingers lacing with hers. "Dinna fash yourself, lass. I'll stay."

She nodded, his warmth seeping in to banish the cold terror that filled her. For a moment she looked deep into his eyes, not certain what she was looking for but positive that she wanted it desperately.

With a sigh, she let her eyes drift shut, taking solace in the fact that, at least for the moment, she was no longer alone.

"*A*h, good, you're awake. I'd begun to think you were going to sleep the day away."

Sunlight washed across the room as Katherine St. Claire pulled the draperies back from the mullioned windows. Ailis blinked in the light and then, despite herself, searched the room for some sign of Ranald.

Katherine's smile deepened. "He's not here."

Her heart twisted, but she tried to ignore the disappointment. There was no real reason for him to have stayed.

"He spent most of the night by your side. Despite my assuring him you had passed the point of danger. But this morning a message arrived for him from Corybrough."

If possible, her heart ached even more. "Is he gone, then?" Her voice was little more than a whisper, and just forming the words seemed to drain her.

Katherine's gaze grew concerned. "No. Not yet. But I fear he might be going soon. He's had word from his father. He's been offered a position in the king's guard."

"At Stirling?" There was no higher honor for a warrior. And Ranald had spent most of his life as a fighting man.

"It would seem so. I don't know all the details. Only what Iain said in passing. I do know that Iain believes it's important to Ranald."

Ailis tried to sit up, wincing at the pain in her head.

"Careful now. It won't do to move too quickly." Katherine shifted to the side of the bed and poured a brownish liquid into a cup, steam rising from the top. "I need you to drink this. The herbs will help with the pain."

Ailis nodded and took the cup, sipping carefully. The bitter brew was soothing in its own way. She took another sip and then moved to set the cup back on the bedside table.

"I need you to drink it all," Katherine said, her tone brooking no argument.

Ailis obediently brought the cup back to her lips. Katherine knew much about herbs and healing. Like most healers she'd learned from her grandmother. But unlike most of them, both Katherine and her Gram were not of this time. And though, in the beginning, Ailis had been astounded by the idea, time and a close relationship with Katherine had made it seem commonplace. Or at least an accepted reality.

She drank deeply, emptying the cup and then looked across the room to where Katherine folded clean linen. "Ranald said he found me." The memories were vague. The mist. The cold. Her fear. And then blessed warmth. Strong arms. Gold-flecked brown eyes.

Sanctuary.

Home.

She shook her head, forcing her foolish thoughts aside, concentrating instead on Katherine's words.

"Yes. In the woods just beyond the river. It was clear that you'd been attacked. But there was no outward sign of struggle."

Ailis shivered.

"I'm sorry." Katherine reached for her hand. "I'm upsetting you."

"No. You've the right of it. I was attacked. But not there. Not in the woods. I honestly have no memory of what happened there. Only that Ranald and his brothers found me." She closed her eyes, reaching again for the memory of his warmth. "Are Benneit and Kendric to go to the king as well?"

"I don't believe so. I think the honor was accorded only to Ranald. He and Iain have fought for him before."

"I remember." She nodded, lifting her gaze to Katherine's. "It was before Iain's father died." The minute the words were out she regretted them. Iain's father, Angus, had been murdered, and her brother had tried to use the fact against Iain. Much to her shame.

"That was a long time ago. Long before I came." Katherine smiled, compassion shining in her eyes. "Anyway, truth be told, I think they both enjoyed the fighting as much as the honor behind it. Men being men and all that."

"Ranald has always had a love for adventure." It was something that had drawn her to him, despite the fact that it meant he never stayed in one place very long. Not that it mattered. "I expect he's quite delighted with the news."

"I suspect as much. Although he's worried about you. He and Iain both."

"But there's no need for concern. The ordeal is over." She shuddered at the memory, her body proving her words a lie.

"Except of course that it isn't," Katherine said, her knowing gaze taking in Ailis' bruised face and battered body. "I know what it feels like to have something like that haunt you. It's almost impossible to truly let it go."

Guilt swelled as Ailis thought of all that her brother had put Katherine through.

Her friend studied her for a moment, then slowly released a breath. "I told them both that you weren't ready to talk about it. That you needed time to recover your strength. But I wonder now if perhaps I spoke in haste." Her hand rested against the gentle swell of her stomach. "Maybe it would be better if you talked with them. Sometimes it's best to just lance the boil."

The analogy wasn't pretty. But then neither were the atrocities of the previous night. If not for herself, she owed it to Jeane, Andro and the others to make sure that the attackers were found and made to pay.

Ailis sucked in a breath, squaring her shoulders. "Can you help me dress?"

~

"And then I ran," Ailis said, lifting a slender shoulder, the only sign of emotion the trembling of her hands. Her face was pale, making the bruises coloring her skin seem that much more horrifying.

The brazier in Iain's work chamber blazed brightly, but Ranald didn't feel the heat. He felt nothing but pure, cold rage. His fists tightened at his side as he fought the urge to cross the room to Ailis' side. He hadn't the right. But she looked so fragile sitting there, firelight turning her long hair to silver. He wished he could take away her pain. More, he wished he could find and destroy those who had hurt her.

"But you didn't recognize anyone?" Iain asked, the tense line of his posture showing his reaction to Ailis' story was much the same as Ranald's.

"Nay," she shook her head. "Although admittedly it was dark and everything happened in a blur. But I promise I'll ne'er forget the face of the man in the abbey." She shuddered, a cloud of fear crossing her face.

Ranald took a step forward, but Katherine, who was sitting next to her, reached for Ailis' hand, the gesture offering comfort.

"We searched the area where Ranald found you," Iain assured her, exchanging a glance with Ranald, "but there was nothing to find."

"Which makes sense," Katherine said, "since the attack actually happened somewhere beyond the abbey."

"And you're certain that everyone is dead?" Iain asked.

"No." Ailis shook her head, wincing with the motion. "Only that Jeane is dead. And that no one came to my aid after my horse threw me off. No one except for Quinn. that is."

"Another fairy," Ranald said with a twisted smile. "I canna believe twice in a lifetime."

"Maybe," Katherine responded, her fingers tightening around Ailis' hand, "but a welcome intervention nevertheless."

"'Tis like the times you rescued me," Iain said, his eyes devouring his wife. Ranald felt a rush of jealousy but pushed the thought aside. He'd made his choices. And besides, hadn't he just been honored by the king?

"She said she was from Tex-ahs," Ailis said, stumbling over the word. "Do you know it, Katherine?"

"I do. It's a long way from where I come from, but part of the same country."

"America," Iain said, nodding as if it were an everyday occurrence for someone from a country that didn't even exist to burst into their world. But, then again, maybe it was.

"Yes." Katherine's smile was only for her husband. As if, for a moment, Ranald and Ailis had ceased to exist.

But then Iain's eyes cleared, and his attention moved back to Ailis. "Did she tell you anything else?"

"No. Nothing. Except that in her time she worked at the abbey. Which is strange I suppose when one considers that even now it is a ruin. She called herself an arc-eol or some such." She looked to Katherine, who had moved to pour herself a cup of wine. "The words had no meaning to me. But mayhap you know them?"

"It's one word actually. But it fits. An archeologist is a person who studies the remnants of the past."

"Well, whoever she is or was, I am grateful," Ranald said before he had a chance to think about the impact of his words.

Ailis sucked in a breath and Katherine smiled.

"What of the men who attacked you in the clearing? I know you said you dinna recognize faces, but what about colors or badges? Was there anything to identify a clan?" Iain asked.

"Not that I could see," Ailis replied, her eyes full of apology. "It was so dark. And I was afraid. The man in the crypt was not wearing a plaid. And he didn't speak as if I were known to him, other than as a target. He mentioned that he wasn't to be paid unless…" She paused, clearly struggling to maintain hold on her emotions. "Unless I was dead," she finished with a defiant lift of her chin.

"So that rules out a random attack. Marauders or the like," Iain said, moving to sit across from Ailis, next to his wife. Anger and frustration kept Ranald pacing back and forth in the space just beyond the chairs.

"What were you thinking, riding through the mountains with such a meager escort?" he asked.

Ailis flinched at the anger in his tone, and Ranald lifted a hand in apology. But she'd come so close to dying.

Eyes glittering, bright pink spots coloring her unbruised skin, Ailis again lifted her chin. Ranald was reminded that she was stronger than she looked. "The laird himself authorized my guard. 'Twas not for me to ask for more men. And besides, I'd no notion anyone would attack. It's not as if my journey was heralded about."

"And yet, clearly, someone knew." Ranald crossed his arms, anger still coloring his words.

"Just because it wasn't bandied about," Iain replied, "does no' mean it was a secret."

"Did you write to someone at Tur nan Clach?" Katherine queried, her brows drawing together in a frown.

"I wrote to my cousin Marsle, but I'd trust her with my life."

"Well, someone betrayed you," Ranald snapped. "The attack was clearly planned. I know the road where it happened. 'Tis narrow and dark. Even in daylight. The perfect place for an ambush."

"As I said, I'll send my men to see to the bodies and check for survivors," Iain replied.

"It's my fault they're dead," Ailis whispered, and this time Ranald didn't hesitate. He strode across the room, reaching for her hand, not giving himself time to question his actions —or his motives.

"'Tis no' your fault, Ailis. You canna have known there would trouble."

"Mayhap, but I should have realized that my presence at Tur nan Clach would be seen by some at least as a threat." She sighed, but didn't pull away from his touch. "I suppose I'd hoped somehow that in the time I was gone things had changed."

"Are any of Alisdair's men still at the holding?" Iain asked.

"I dinna know." Ailis frowned. "I know that Manus Macaidie and Uncle Lyall were allies of a sort. Which means that he could have weaseled his way into a position of power again."

"Macaidie," Iain repeated. "Alisdair's right-hand man. He was away when Alisdair…" He faltered, his gaze moving to his wife. "When he tried to hurt Katherine."

Ailis blanched, her discomfort evident. "I'm so sorry."

"'Twas no' your fault," Ranald was quick to say, his fingers tightening around hers as he cursed Alisdair for the bastard that he was.

"The important thing is that you didn't see Manus Macaidie. In the woods, I mean." Katherine leaned back against her husband.

"No, and I am certain I'd have recognized him." Fear and revulsion tracked across Ailis' face.

Ranald pushed to his feet again, anger resurfacing as he

thought about the horrors of Ailis' young life. "If he is behind this, I swear I will kill him."

"I canna argue with you there, Cousin," Iain said. "But Ailis is tiring. And I dinna think we're gaining anything in prolonging the discussion. We'll know more after we've sent men to the abbey."

"You're right of course." He shot a look at Ailis, noticing that her cheeks were even more ashen and her body tight with tension. "You need rest. I am to leave for court in a day or so. If you'd grant me the honor, I'll see you safely back to Moy."

"No." The word was sharp and, irrationally, disappointment speared his gut. She paused, her gaze colliding with his. "What I mean to say is that, while your offer is appreciated, I cannot accept. I am not going back to Moy."

"Of course not," Katherine soothed, shooting an angry look in Ranald's direction. "You'll stay here for as long as you like. Until you feel strong enough to face the journey."

Again, Ailis shook her head. "I thank you for the welcome, but I canna stay here either. My place is at Tur nan Clach. Now more than ever."

"But if the attack was predicated on your return, then you won't be safe there," Katherine protested.

"Perhaps not, but Tur nan Clach is my home. And with my uncle's death, the responsibility of its people falls to me. I will not shirk my duty."

"Even if it gets you killed?" Ranald asked, striving for a calm he did not feel. "Surely you canna mean to put your life at risk again?"

Fire shot from her eyes, her determination clear. "I mean exactly that. I appreciate the care you've given me. All of you. But I'll no' be wrapped in a wee bairn's blanket. I'm a woman grown. And I will see to my holding."

Even as he opened his mouth to argue, Ranald could not

fault the lass. Were it his holding, he'd feel the same. "Fine, then," he said, the words sounding harsher than intended. "But you'll no' go without escort."

"Iain will provide men," Katherine offered, her eyes narrowing as she met her husband's reluctant gaze. "Won't you, my love?"

With an apologetic glance in Ranald's direction, he acquiesced. "Of course. I would go myself, but as you can see Katherine nears her confinement, and I canna be away from her. Still, my men are yours to command."

"There are not words enough to thank you." Ailis squared her shoulders, offering a smile.

Ranald swallowed a groan, knowing it was pointless to argue. Her mind was made up. And he'd known her long enough now to understand that she wouldn't change it. "If you'll provide a few men, Iain, I can provide escort."

Ailis frowned. "But I thought you'd been called to the king. Surely you must answer the summons. Being part of the king's guard is everything you've dreamed of."

"'Tis no' more important than your safety." He fought to keep his expression neutral, rocked by the emotions she pulled from him. "The king will simply have to wait."

CHAPTER 4

"*H*ave you gone soft in the head then, *bràthair?*"Kendric asked Ranald as the three brothers grouped themselves around the fire in the great hall. "All of your life you've relished naught more than fighting. And to be assigned the king's guard—'tis a grand honor. And no' one to take lightly."

"And to turn it away on account of a wee sprite of a lass who hasn't a chance in the world of taking Tur nan Clach," Benneit inserted with a growl. "'Tis a proposition finished before 'tis even begun. Even if Duncan Mackintosh, the head of all of Chattan, mind, had backed her fully 'twould be an uphill battle. But without his support, what makes you believe she has a chance of succeeding?"

Ranald drained his cup of ale, his gaze meeting both of his brothers'. "I am no' going to turn down the king. Only postpone my acceptance a wee bit."

"But why?" Kendric asked, throwing up his hands in frustration. "Surely you canna think you'll gain anything for your bother. Benneit is right. If Duncan cared, he would no' have sent her with only a handful of guards."

"Are you sweet on the lass, then?" Benneit's eyes narrowed as he studied his brother.

"Of course not," Ranald snapped, aware that he was perhaps protesting a bit too vehemently.

Kendric's arched brows indicated that he entertained the same thought. "'Twould no' be a surprise. The lass is comely —although a bit skinny for my taste."

"She might be tiny, but she has courage to spare. You wouldn't believe the hell her brother put her through." Even Ranald didn't know the whole of it, but she'd shared a little bit. And he'd been part of the group of men who discovered her locked inside a cage in her brother's cellar. The thought of all that she'd been through angered him even now that it was only memory.

"Aye, but thanks to you I've an idea of it," Benneit said, lifting a hand in peace. "Still, that past combined with the reality of the attack in the woods…" He trailed off, his expression turning apologetic. "Sometimes stupidity masquerades as bravery."

"Ailis is not stupid. Nor is she acting without thought. She loves her holding and its people. She wants what is best for them. You canna fault her for that."

"I dinna." Benneit shook his head. "But wanting something is no' the same as making it so. And this isn't your fight, bràthair."

"Mayhap no'. But I canna leave her on her own. I canna turn my back, knowing that in so doing I might be putting her in danger."

"I ask again, what is this woman to you?" Frustration colored Kendric's voice, mirroring the feelings warring inside of Ranald.

He wasn't sure he had an answer for his brother's question. He wanted to say it was chivalry. The need to protect a woman—any woman. But somewhere deep inside he knew it was more. Ailis truly did love Tur nan Clach. And if he were the kind of man to attach himself to a place—surely he'd do anything to fight for it, too.

But he wasn't that kind of man.

Still...

"I know how much her brother's betrayals cost her. Not just what he did to her, but also to Katherine and Iain. And to weaker members of her clan. She feels responsible. And under her uncle, things were no' much better. So I understand her need to stand and fight. And I canna in good conscience let her go it alone."

"But she would no' be on her own. Iain promised some of his men."

"Who are loyal to Iain first. She needs warriors of her own. Even if only temporarily."

Benneit sighed, tipping his mug and draining the last of his ale. "Right then, I suppose we're headed for Tur nan Clach."

"You dinna have to come with me," Ranald protested.

Kendric's expression darkened to a scowl. "You were just lecturing us about the obligations to family. Ailis isn't the only one connected to her kin. Where you go, we go."

"What he means," Benneit said with a crooked smile, "is that he's no' ready to go home and face our mother yet. Better to follow you on your misguided quest. Someone's got to watch out for yer arse. After all, 'tis been promised in service to the king."

"He'll no' be happy with the delay," Kendric observed.

"Aye, well, he'll no' have a choice. And who's to say when I actually received the summons?"

"Yer playin' with fire, little brother," Benneit said. "Nevertheless, you can count on us. We'll have your back. And that of yer fair maiden, too."

"I told you, she is no' mine," Ranald protested, not certain why his brothers continued to dig at him. He was only stepping in where needed. "'Tis Iain I'm helping. Despite his words to the contrary, he'd have felt bound to go—even with Katherine's confinement."

Kendric's smile was slow. "Keep telling yourself that, *bràthair*. And maybe if you say it often enough, you'll actually convince yourself 'tis true."

～

*A*ilis stared out the window of the solar at the falling snow. The flakes spiraled and twirled, illuminated by the braziers in the inner courtyard. Behind her, in the fireplace, an ember popped, and despite the chamber's warmth she shivered. The holding was quiet. The house abed. But even though weary to the bone, she'd been unable to sleep.

She closed her eyes for a moment, wrapping her arms around her waist, seeing again the slaughter in the woods. Jeane, Andro, the others. Strangers all. Nevertheless, because of her, they were dead. Iain's men had found their bodies in the woods where she'd fled, left lying where they'd fallen. There'd been no trace of the men who had killed them. At least now the dead could rest in peace. Buried amidst the beauty of the mountain forest. It should have been a comforting thought, but it wasn't.

There'd been no sign of Quinn or Ailis' attacker at the abbey either, but they'd found her torn cloak and seen signs of the struggle. Her head throbbed and she swallowed rising bile, the memory of the man's fetid breath sending shudders wracking through her body.

She'd come so close to death. And yet here she stood. Alive. Once again she'd survived. But at what cost? More people were dead. Would the curse of being a Davidson never end?

With Iain's help, she'd sent word of the attack to the Laird of Chattan. Duncan Mackintosh would not be happy with the outcome of her bid for freedom. But the knowledge only made her more firm in her commitment to make her way to Tur nan Clach.

Surely there'd be some welcome there? Not every clansman had supported her brother and her uncle. And with both of them gone, there'd be room for change. She was determined now, more than ever, to stand strong. To honor her mother's memory. To make up for the years of hardship and pain her clan had endured at the hands of the Davidsons.

Although Cairstine Dow had died when Ailis was very young, Ailis still had vague memories. Her mother had been as ethereal as a sprite, and her love for her clan had been matched only by her husband's revulsion for it.

Ailis' father had never loved anything. Or anyone. Certainly not his lady or her people. Forced into marriage, Col Davidson had never accepted his lot in life. Believing until his death, that he was better than anything Tur nan Clach had to offer. Anything Cairstine or their children had to offer. And Alisdair had absorbed their father's hatred and spewed it back ten-fold.

She shivered again, opening her eyes, surprised to feel the wet kiss of tears as they slid down her face. Angrily, she brushed them away as she watched the soft fall of snow. A woman's tears only made her weak. She'd been taught that lesson as a child. And had it reinforced in the dungeons of Tur nan Clach.

A noise had her spinning around, still wiping her face.

"I dinna mean to frighten you," Ranald said, coming to a halt in the doorway. "I had no idea anyone was still awake."

She dropped her hand, lifting her chin. "I couldn't sleep."

"Nor could I." He stepped into the firelight and she swallowed, forcing herself not to take a step in retreat. The shadows made him seem larger somehow. Harder. And yet, even with the flickering light, she could see concern reflected in the depths of his gaze. She'd fallen half in love with him when she'd first stayed here at Duncreag. Despite his towering height and brawny build, he'd been kind to her. Made her laugh. Made her feel safe. Made her feel things she couldn't admit—even to herself.

But Ranald Macqueen was a rogue through and through. And told the stories to prove it. Besides, even a man as seemingly kind as Ranald wasn't to be completely trusted. Ailis had spent most of her life at the mercy of men, and she'd not give herself to another. No matter how much his eyes reminded her of the blue-green waters of a rushing burn.

"If you'd rather be alone..." He gestured to the door behind him.

She opened her mouth, thinking to send him away, but instead waved toward the cushioned bench between the window and the fire. "I've been watching the snow," she said, turning back to the window and the icy ground beyond. "It makes everything look so fresh. So innocent."

"But looks can be deceiving." Ignoring the offered seat, he moved instead to stand behind her. She caught her breath, his heat and strength seeming to surround her even though they were not touching.

"Aye." She nodded, still looking out at the falling snow. It glistened in the half light. "Even amongst beauty there can be terror." She shivered and wrapped her arms around herself.

"There's no need to be afraid. You're safe here." He stepped closer. "With me. With Iain."

"I know," she said. "But I canna hide away here forever."

"I understand why you want to go back to Tur nan Clach, Ailis. I even admire your determination. But you have nothing to prove. What happened out there wasn't your fault. Any more than your brother's sins are yours. No one expects you to make reparations."

"I expect it of myself, Ranald." She turned then, tipping her head to look up at him, a shiver of something besides fear working its way up her spine.

"And I admire you for your courage, lass. But I canna countenance why you'd willingly put yourself in danger."

"I've spent most of my life afraid, waiting for someone to come and rescue me. I think perhaps the time has come to rescue myself. To prove once and for all that I'm stronger than my brother and those who followed him. That I'll not be frightened away."

Even as she said the words, doubt edged with fear threatened to swamp her. She swallowed, her gaze trapped by his.

"Well, I will no' let you do this on your own." She started to protest but he raised a hand, his strong fingers brushing back a strand of her hair. "I'm no' saying you canna do this by yourself, Ailis. I'm saying you dinna have to."

She leaned into the warmth of his touch, relishing the connection, drawing from his strength. Then, with a soft sigh, she tensed to pull away. But his fingers moved to circle the back of her head and he pulled her closer, bending his head, his lips brushing against hers. Once and then again.

"Ach, Ailis," Ranald groaned, pulling her closer, deepening the kiss.

Somewhere in her rational mind she knew she should pull free. That being here alone with him risked more than she was willing to give. But it felt so good to be held. To feel safe. To feel desired. After everything that had happened, surely she was allowed one moment of weakness.

"Open for me, lass." His voice was low, almost guttural, and instinctively she did as he asked, his tongue sweeping inside her mouth, taking possession.

His hands moved to her back and then her waist, pulling her closer. She could smell leather and horse. Soap and something uniquely Ranald. He tasted of ale and spice. And she found herself wanting more. Wanting him. Even as she wondered exactly what that would entail.

Though she was a maiden, thanks to her brother, she felt far from innocent. And yet, she had never experienced anything like this. The feel of his lips and hands went beyond mere pleasure. It was transcendent. Although even as she had the thought she wondered if kissing him had made her feeble-minded.

Her knees grew weak, her breath coming in shortened gasps. Deep inside she felt heavy and hot. His lips slid from her mouth to her cheeks and then her eyelids. She shivered as he kissed the soft whorl of her ear, his mouth warm and wet against her skin.

His slid his hands upward, circling her ribcage, his thumbs reverently stroking the swell of her breasts. She moaned and pressed herself closer. How different it was to be held with a tender touch.

His mouth moved back to her lips, his kiss gentle.

And it was the touch of emotion that jerked her free of her dreaming.

"I canna," she said, pulling free, even as a part of her longed to step back into the warmth of his embrace. "We canna. You belong at Sterling with the king. And I belong at Tur nan Clach. There is no room for anything more."

"I will no' apologize. I dinna regret a thing, Ailis. You're a brave and beautiful woman. But I'll honor your wishes and no' press you for more."

"Thank you." The words were low, almost inaudible, and she fought against a wave of regret. Surely it was the stress of the past few days. Her brush with death. 'Twas to be expected. Ranald was not the kind of man a woman could easily ignore.

"But even if you insist there be nothing more between us," he was saying, his eyes narrowed as he crossed his arms over his massive chest, "I'm still coming with you on the morrow. And nothing you say will change my mind."

For a moment she thought to argue. To insist that she didn't need anyone. But even as she had the thought, she knew she was being daft. She did need protection. She needed him. Not that she'd ever admit as much.

"Fine, then. I will allow it."

"Very well, my lady." He swept into a courtly bow. "I live to serve." As he straightened, the twitching of his lips gave lie to the serious tone of his voice.

She crossed her arms over her breasts. "All I ask is that you keep your hands to yourself." She wasn't certain if she was speaking to him or to herself, but either way she knew she spoke true. Men were not to be trusted. Even when they seemed like they truly cared.

"As you wish." He inclined his head, but not before she saw the heat ignite in his eyes.

She swallowed, an answering warmth spearing deep inside her, and as she turned back to the window she couldn't help wondering if perhaps they'd opened a door that would best have been left closed.

CHAPTER 5

"You don't have to go anywhere, you know," Katherine looked up at Ailis, one hand shading her eyes against the rising sun. "You can stay here with us. Be here when my baby is born."

The idea was tempting. Katherine had been more of a friend to her than almost anyone she'd ever known. For a moment her thoughts moved to Quinn. The woman had saved her from certain death. And perhaps even more so from something far worse. Two women who had been there when she needed someone. Two women who each came from another time.

'Twas impossible to ken something so beyond belief, and yet here Katherine stood, proof that such a thing was indeed possible. Perhaps Duncreag was enchanted—but that would mean that the abbey, too, was under the spell.

Ailis shook her head, tightened her hands on the reins, and smiled down at her friend. "I canna stay. As much as I'd like to. I canna. I belong at Tur nan Clach. As surely as you belong here at Duncreag. It remains to be seen whether it will work. But I have to try."

"I understand." Katherine reached up to squeeze her hand, Ailis' horse shifting impatiently. "I just don't want you to suffer any more than you already have. You deserve happiness, Ailis." She glanced at Ranald, who was standing beside his horse, talking with Iain.

"I do," she replied, following Katherine's gaze. "But I'm afraid it doesn't lie in that direction. Ranald is not the kind of man to settle down. And I have other more important things that require my attention."

"Nothing is more important than love, Ailis." She dropped her hand to the curve of her swelling belly.

Ahead of her, Ranald vaulted onto his horse, Beithir. "Are we ready then, lads?" he called to his brothers. The inky black stallion tossed his head; like his master, clearly ready to be off.

Ranald had kept a polite distance since they'd broken their fast. Ailis told herself that it was as it should be. That he was only following her own dictate. But somewhere deep inside she recognized that she was disappointed at the ease with which he'd been able to dismiss last night's passion.

But then, 'twas only a passing fancy for him.

And for her, too. She squared her shoulders and avoided Katherine's knowing gaze.

"I canna argue with your thinking, *mo chridhe*," Iain said, coming to stand beside his wife, his arm around her shoulders. "There is truly nothing that matters more than love. Ailis, I wish you well. And Katherine is right. You always have a home here with us should you desire it."

Tears pricked at the back of her eyes and she sucked in a breath, forcing a smile. "There are no words to express how very much that means to me."

"And if we dinna get an early start, we will no' make it to Bealag's by nightfall," Ranald cautioned.

They were to break their journey at the home of the

Macqueen brothers' old nurse. When the boys had left the nursery, the woman had married Effric Abernathy, one of Iain's father's clansmen.

"I canna wait to see the old woman," Kendric said, his horse dancing with impatience.

"I doubt that she'll feel the same way about you," Benneit replied with a grin. "Particularly if she remembers the time you left a toad in her shoe."

"I dinna think anyone could scream that loud," Kendric laughed. "I very much doubt that she's forgotten."

"Or forgiven." Ranald waggled his eyebrows at his brother.

And Ailis felt suddenly all alone. Surrounded by people who cared, but none of them her own kin. Her own people. If for no other reason than that, she needed to go home. To try to make her own place in the world. To be where she truly belonged.

"Safe journey, then," Katherine said, still nestled against Iain's shoulder. "Send word that all is well. And Ranald, see that you take care of Ailis."

"Aye, you can count on it," he replied, urging Beithir forward until he was by her side, their horses close enough that Ranald's thigh was warm against her leg. "And know that once we reach Tur nan Clach, I'll no' be leavin' Ailis until I'm certain she's found whatever it is that she seeks." His words were meant to reassure Katherine, but his gaze collided with Ailis', and she shivered as if he'd touched her. It felt as if he were making her a silent promise. As if somehow he knew all that lay deep in her heart.

The idea should have frightened her, but instead, for the first time in forever, she felt a small tug of hope.

*A*ilis rode beneath the bare canopy of the trees, the winter wind whistling through the branches. The snow had almost melted, the noonday sun cutting through the haze of clouds, but the world still felt as if it were shrouded in gray.

Ahead of her, Ranald rode with his brothers, laughing at something Kendric said. Behind her a small cadre of Iain's men followed. Fergus Mackintosh and Roger Macbean were arguing about something, but that, in and of itself, was nothing new. The two men were old friends, but still considered themselves rivals in service to Iain, their laird.

William Macgowen rode forward, pulling his horse alongside hers. A young man on the cusp of adulthood, William was dedicated to Katherine and Iain—emphasis on Katherine. A year ago, she'd used her healing skills to save his life when a battle injury had threatened to take it. He followed her now like an overgrown puppy, and Ailis suspected that his assignment as part of her guard was, in part, an attempt to give Katherine a much-needed break from his devotion.

He smiled at her in apology. "I dinna mean to invade yer privacy, but I canna stand the two of them bickering any longer." He tilted his head toward Roger and Fergus, still arguing behind him.

"What are they going on about then?" Ailis asked, masking a smile.

"The merits of fighting with a claymore and a short sword. Fergus swears 'tis no other way to battle, and Roger is equally certain that a man fares better with only the broad sword."

"And you, William? What do you think?"

The young man frowned as he considered the question, freckles standing out against his fair skin. "I suppose it all depends on the man. There are those that have the skill to fight with two weapons, and those who are strong enough to make do with just the one."

"How very tactful of you to put it that way," Ailis replied, "but your words remind me that there is a third option as well."

William's brows drew together with curiosity. "And what, pray tell, would that be?"

"Why, to solve the conflict without any weapons at all, of course."

For a moment he looked confused, and then his eyes brightened as he grinned. "Ye mean a man might manage to avoid fighting."

"Using the right words, aye. 'Tis called diplomacy. And with a silver tongue and a quick mind, someone like you could easily put both Fergus and Roger to shame."

William's neck and cheeks reddened, the color at odds with the fiery orange of his hair. "I canna be sure that I'd be so quick to think in the face o' danger, but I do thank ye for the compliment."

"Katherine has told me of your bravery in battle," Ailis said. "And the injury you sustained at the hands of my brother." It seemed she was always faced with the fallout from Alisdair's maneuverings. "I'm sorry you fell victim to his treachery."

"No more than ye did, my lady," William assured her, his gaze sobering with the thought. "I canna countenance a man who would hurt his own sister. Forgive me for saying so, but 'tis best for all of us that he is gone."

"There's nothing to forgive. Alisdair made his own bed, so to speak. I canna find it in my heart to be sorry that he is dead."

"I should no' have brought it up." He looked decidedly

uncomfortable, and Ailis regretted that she'd caused his unease.

"William, you did nothing wrong," she reassured him. "'Twas I who spoke of my brother. And I've taken no offense at your words, I assure you."

"Still, if I brought you discomfort, I dinna mean to do so."

They rode for a bit in silence, then William turned to meet her gaze. "If you don't mind my asking, why, after everything that's happened, would you wish to return to Tur nan Clach?"

"I need to make it right." The words seemed overly simple. As if she could wave a magic wand and make all of the pain and suffering her clan had endured under servitude to her menfolk simply disappear. If only it were that easy.

"But yer a woman," William said with a puzzled frown, clearly oblivious to the insult he'd just leveled.

"Never underestimate the power of a woman, lad."

Ailis struggled to contain her horse, both of them startled by Ranald's silent approach.

"They have a well of strength, William, that we can only begin to understand. And I can tell you from experience that, although Ailis may appear to be a mere wisp of a lass, she's made of far sterner stuff. Her clan will be lucky to have her watching o'er them."

It was Ailis' turn to feel the hot wash of a blush.

"I canna seem to help but shove my foot in it every chance I get," William said, his discomfort readily apparent. "Ailis, I was no' meaning offense. Only that 'tis hard enough to run a clan as a man. I'd no' want to try to do it as a woman."

"William, you're no' helping," Ranald offered, eyebrows raised.

"Aye, I ken that. Mayhap 'twould be better if I just kept

my mouth shut." With that he allowed his horse to fall back, leaving Ranald and Ailis more or less on their own.

"The lad meant no harm," Ranald said, his gaze filled with concern.

"I know that. And he's certainly no' the first man to question the ability of a woman to lead." She paused, looking up at the gray shrouded sky. "I know it will be difficult to take control. I even ken that it could be impossible. But I have to try."

"I canna pretend that it would no' be easier if you had a man at your side."

"Are you offering to fill the position, then?" she queried, biting back a smile even as she smothered a surge of longing.

"'Tis of no matter if I am or not. After last night you made it bloody well clear that you wouldn't consider it if I were."

His fierce gaze locked with hers, and her body tightened in anticipation of...well, she wasn't exactly sure. But she was wise enough to know that if she gave whatever it was enough rein, it would have the power to consume her.

"But you're not." She narrowed her eyes, daring him to answer differently—confused as to why she cared.

"Nay. I'm no'."

Her heart sank, but she pasted on a smile nevertheless. "This is a ridiculous conversation. As soon as I've arrived safely at Tur nan Clach, you'll be bound for Stirling and the king. As I said last night, our lives are moving in different directions."

"That they are," Ranald agreed, and she fought another wave of disappointment.

Surely she was only worrying about being on her own again. The thought of last night's kiss and embrace was nothing more than a memory. One she'd carry with her always, but never allow herself to turn into more than it was.

"I think we should stop to rest the horses," Kendric said,

dropping back to ride beside them. "'Tis past midday, and best that we break for food and other," he shot a sideways glance at Ailis, "necessities."

She opened her mouth to argue, but in truth her head hurt and her other injuries ached from the jarring ride. Katherine had warned her it was too soon to travel, but the need to press on had overridden her friend's concern.

"Are you well, lass?" Ranald asked, his face reflecting his concern as she tightened her hands on the reins.

"Aye." She forced herself to straighten, lifting her chin. "But a wee rest would not be amiss."

"We'll stop ahead near the burn, then," Ranald called to his brother, gesturing for the men behind to follow as they left the trail. "The trees will offer at least a modicum of protection."

He pulled ahead of her, and Ailis told herself she was grateful for the interruption. If for no other reason, she couldn't afford the distraction. She'd set her mind to righting her brother's wrongs, and nothing could be allowed to get in her way. Not the threat of attack, nor the pain in her head.

Not even the man whose mere presence made her blood heat and her heart sing.

~

Ranald watched the men as they watered their horses and ate Flora's bannocks and oatcakes. As cold as it was, they didn't dare risk a fire for fear that someone was watching. They'd seen no sign that they were being followed, but then he and his brothers hadn't survived all these years by throwing caution to the wind.

"Just a wee bit longer and we'll be off again," Benneit said, clearly of the same mind as Ranald.

"Aye. I canna say that stopping even this long makes me

comfortable, but thanks to her injuries Ailis is in pain and no doubt in need of relief."

"She's not the only one," Fergus said, emerging from behind an evergreen, straightening his plaid. "Where's she gone off to then?"

"Just beyond the rocks." Ranald gestured to a tumble of stone flanking the rushing burn. Conifers grew from the scree, their branches stretching upward, green fronds waving in the cold wind.

"I'm surprised you dinna follow her," Kendric said, emerging from another stand of trees. "Despite yer protestations to the contrary, you seem to be overly cautious when it comes to her safety."

"Mayhap, but she deserves a wee bit of privacy as well, and I can see the rocks from here."

"Aye, but you canna see what is on the other side o' the burn." Fergus' words, as usual, were caustic at best. The old man was always the last one to see the bright side of any situation.

"There are near to twenty men in this clearing," Kendric observed. "An attacker would be a fool to risk anything against those odds."

"Unless he had more men or better access to his goal." Fergus shrugged.

Ranald's hand closed around the hilt of his claymore, but he held his ground. Ailis needed some time to herself, and she'd not thank him for charging in to witness her ablutions. Still, Fergus had the right of it. Better to act with care.

"I'll check on her." He strode through the trees, not waiting for a response from his brothers. He focused on the pile of rocks, eyes searching for a spot of color, the dark purple of her cloak or the silvery white of her hair. He told himself that there was no cause for worry, but his fist tightened on the hilt of his sword.

The winter-bare brush grew more dense as he neared the burn, gnarled branches grabbing at his plaid and cloak as he passed. Fighting his way through the stand of pines, he burst into a small clearing. Ailis was kneeling beside the burn, her long hair obscuring her face.

"Ailis," he called, "are you all right, lass?"

In answer she held out her hands, the skin stained with blood.

"You've hurt your hands." Closing the distance between them, he dropped to his knees beside her, brushing back her hair with one hand.

"No. The blood is from my head. I grew dizzy and lost my balance." She lifted her face, her bruised cheek seeming even more purple beneath the winter sun. Blood seeped from the wound just above her temple. "I'm sorry." She brushed it with her hand, wincing at the contact. "I can't seem to get it to stop." Her eyes filled with tears and she swallowed against obvious pain.

Ranald reached beneath his plaid and tore a strip of linen from the bottom of his *léine*. He tore it in two and folded the longer piece until it formed a pad. "Let me help you."

Taking the old bandage from her shaking fingers, he dipped it into the cold rushing water, holding it there until most of the dried blood had washed away. Then, carefully, he began to sponge the wound. "I know it hurts," he said. "But I need to get it clean."

She nodded, closing her eyes against the discomfort as he worked, her muscles tightening with the effort. "Good lass," he murmured. "Almost there." He continued to clean, prodding and probing only when absolutely necessary, and then sat back on his haunches. "All done. Do you have the salve that Katherine gave you?"

Her eyes fluttered open, her chin lifting as she met his gaze with a nod. She barely moved as she reached inside her cloak to produce a small box from the pocket sewn there. His gut churned as he watched her fight against the pain. "Here," she whispered, holding it out with a shaking hand. "I'd forgotten."

His heart swelled with something he wasn't ready to put a name to as he reached out to take the box, his big hand engulfing hers. For a moment they sat, gazes locked, communicating without words. And then Ranald shook his head, pulling himself from his flight of fancy as he took the box and opened it, dipping his fingers into the pungent mixture. "This will no doubt hurt a bit. But only for a moment."

"Just do it," she said, chin set, eyes narrowed, her emotions clearly back in control.

Gently, he spread the salve across her brow and then pressed the improvised pad against the wound, securing it with the other half of the strip of linen. "'Tis no' as good as Katherine's work, but for now it will have to do. The bleeding has already started to slow."

"Thank you," she said with a faint smile. "I should have been more careful."

"You're hurt. And you've pressed yourself more than you should have. Katherine said it was too soon for you to travel." The minute the words were out he wished them back, even though he spoke the truth.

Her eyes flashed first with anger and then something akin to regret. "You've the right of it, of course. I've always been too stubborn to listen to reason. But I was afraid if I didn't go now, I never would. Despite my love for my clan, I realize that there is danger in returning." She waved at her bandaged head. "I know that there are those who would see me dead."

"You must know that as long as there is breath in my body, I'll no' let anything happen to you. And my brothers feel the same."

"I canna say that I understand why you're willing to take

the risk, but I am grateful nevertheless. With you here, I am not so afraid."

He reached out again to smooth back her hair, running his fingers along the soft shell of her ear as he tucked the strand behind it. "In truth, Ailis," he said, "I think you are perhaps one of the bravest lasses I've ever known."

She sucked in a ragged breath and he leaned forward, desire building as his lips met hers. An inner voice insisted that this wasn't the time or the place but he ignored it, pulling her closer instead, his hands gentle as he cradled her face. There was just something about her that called to him. Always had. Probably always would.

She issued a soft moan and pushed closer, her hands moving to tangle in his hair. The kiss deepened, and for a moment Ranald lost all rational thought. There was nothing but the feel and smell of her as she opened her mouth and their tongues danced together.

"Ranald."

The name split the quiet of the clearing and they jerked apart, Ailis breathing hard, her eyes wide. She lifted a hand to her mouth as he pushed to his feet and turned away from her, positioning his body to protect her as she rose behind him.

"*Bràthair*," Kendric called, moving through the bushes into the clearing. "I dinna mean to intrude, but we've got company.

Ranald's hand moved to his sword even as he swung out his arm to draw Ailis against his side. "Enemy or friend?"

"'Tis yet to be determined." Before Kendric could say anything more, the pine trees shook again as three men pushed into the clearing.

"I bid them to wait," Benneit said, his eyes narrowed in anger. "But this one refused. Insisted he needed to be sure Ailis was unharmed."

"And just who is he to be asking?" Ranald demanded, glaring across at the older of three men. He stood almost as tall as Ranald and his brothers. Their elder by maybe ten years. Still, there was nothing soft about the man. His hair was reddish brown. Long and tangled. His eyes were a steely gray, his mouth curled into a snarl when he caught sight of Ailis.

"Manus Macaidie," the man replied, lifting a dirk. "Now let go of what is mine." Both Kendric and Benneit reached for their swords as the second man pulled his as well.

Ailis shuddered and pressed closer. Ranald squeezed her waist and then pushed her behind him as he, too, drew his weapon. "I ken who you are," he said, holding the older man's gaze. "And I can say with certainty that you have no claim on Ailis. So I don't believe I'll be turning her over to the likes of you. How am to know that you're no' the man who tried to kill her?"

"Because I'm her betrothed."

"No," Ailis whispered, the protest issued with equal parts fear and anger. And then she stepped up beside Ranald, lifting her gaze to meet Macaidie's. Clearly anger had won out. "'Tis impossible for you to be anything to me," she spat. "But most clearly you are not my betrothed."

"I've approval from the Laird of Chattan. I act on his orders."

"You mistake my words. I am not asking how you came to claim this right. I am telling you 'tis no' possible." Her hand slipped into Ranald's, her chin tilting with defiance. "For I canna marry you when I am already wed."

CHAPTER 6

*S*ilence stretched through the clearing, the only sound the rushing burn behind them. Ailis felt the blood pounding in her head and fear curling in her belly. What in the world had possessed her to say that she was wed?

"And who, then, have ye taken to yer bed?" Manus snarled, anger making him take a step forward.

Ranald growled a warning and moved closer to Ailis. Both of Ranald's brothers closed on either side, brandishing their weapons. She was grateful for their support, but not as certain that they would stand by her when she answered Manus' question.

Sucking in a deep breath, she tightened her fingers around Ranald's arm and prayed that he'd understand. "I am newly wed to the man you see before you. Ranald Macqueen is my husband, and you'd do well to mind the truth of it." Ailis was relieved that her voice held steady.

"When did this happen?" Manus demanded.

"Last eve," Ailis said. "We're on our way to Tur nan Clach with the news."

"It canna be," Manus replied. "I have the laird's word on it."

"His word is worth less than nothing, then," Ranald said, slipping his arm around Ailis' waist, his sword still raised. "For I take Ailis to be my wife."

"And I stand as witness," Kendric was quick to add.

Ailis shivered with the enormity of what she was asking of them.

"Me, as well," Benneit echoed. "I witness their troth."

The fact that they all spoke in present tense did not escape her. They were sealing the bond. Ranald's grip tightened. "I tell you now, Manus, you can no' have what already belongs to me."

Fergus, William, and Roger stepped into the little clearing, weapons drawn, several of Iain's men just behind them.

Manus surveyed the group through narrowed eyes, clearly recognizing that the odds were not in his favor. "I have arrived too late, it appears, to claim my bride." His heavy gaze moved from Ailis' head to her toes as though he were touching her. She shuddered and moved closer to Ranald. "You're a lucky bastard, Macqueen."

"Aye, that I am."

"Ye say yer on your way to Tur nan Clach. Let me offer to escort you. I left the rest of my men in the clearing."

"There's less than ten of them," William offered, shooting a disgusted look in Manus' direction.

"I thank you for the offer," Ranald nodded, "but we break tonight at the home of an old friend. So there's no need to accompany us."

"Aye, but there is," Manus insisted. "You said yourself that someone wants the lass dead. And I can see for myself that she has been injured." He frowned, eyes narrowing. "Mayhap she wasn't in her right mind when she agreed to wed you."

"I may have been injured, but I know my own mind." Ailis

fought again to keep her voice steady, anger mixing with trepidation.

"And she chose me." Ranald moved closer, his strength banishing her fear. "We need nothing more from you."

"Ah, but you do," Manus said, a sly smile lifting the corner of his lips. "The laird also named me head of Clan Davidson."

"But it is my place to lead," Ailis protested. "They're my people, not yours."

"And where have you been these last few months, while yer uncle lay dying?" Manus growled, taking a threatening step forward, anger playing across his weathered face. "Playing at court in Moy? Enticing the likes of him to yer bed?"

"Watch your mouth," Ranald snapped, eyes narrowing. "You're talking to a lady."

"You forget I've known Ailis," his mouth twisted into a sneer as his gaze lingered on her breasts, "for most of her life. And since she is my kin I'm bound to protect her, wedded or no'. Until she's safely returned to Tur nan Clach, I'll no' be leaving her on her own. Especially if all she has to protect her is the likes o' you."

Ailis felt Ranald's muscles tighten in anger and she laid a hand on his arm. Better to placate the man and give themselves time to regroup.

"Suit yourself," Ranald said, the tension in his arms and shoulders at odds with the casual tone of his voice. "I canna stop you from traveling the same road. But I warn you to leave Ailis be."

"Well now, mayhap we should leave that to the lady herself," Manus said as he stepped forward again, two of his men moving with him as others stepped into the clearing.

Ranald lifted his sword, his gaze moving from Manus to his brothers. Ailis' tightened her hand on his arm. As much as she hated Manus, she couldn't countenance the idea that her rash pronouncement might lead to blood being spilled—to Ranald or his brothers being injured or worse. There could be no good come from engaging Manus and his men.

"I have all that I want right here," she replied, head held high, her gaze locking with Manus'. "There's no need for you to stay. But as you say, we come from the same place." She couldn't bring herself to call the man kin. "So if you insist, I suppose 'tis only right to accept your offer of added protection."

"I'll leave my best men with you."

"You're not staying, then?" Ailis asked.

"Nay. I must return to Tur nan Clach with the news. There'll be much to see to before yer arrival."

"We've no need of anything from you," Ranald spat, his eyes narrowed in anger.

"Make no mistake, Macqueen," the other man taunted, his gaze moving slowly from Ranald back to Ailis. "I always take care of what is mine."

~

"Married?" Bealag Abernathy exclaimed, her eyes widening in surprise. "Merciful heavens, I had no idea. Your mother didn't think to write me." The older woman narrowed her eyes, searching his face. Bea had always known when Ranald or his brothers were stretching the truth.

Although, in point of fact, he wasn't actually lying. For better or worse, he and Ailis were in fact now man and wife. They'd pledged themselves in front of witnesses. Albeit in a moment of crisis. Still, Highland law would prevail. The bond was set. And although it was not impossible to undo what had been done, he wasn't a man to make a commitment lightly.

Of course, he should be angry, or at least frustrated at Ailis's duplicity. But instead he felt oddly protective, and if he were being honest, strangely euphoric. As if he'd captured an elusive prize.

"Mother, ah, does no' actually ken," he admitted, feeling a wave of guilt. Unwarranted guilt. He'd been nothing but a gentleman. And it wasn't as if he'd coerced Ailis into marriage. Quite the opposite actually. Still, standing there beneath the weight of Bea's questioning stare, he found himself shifting on his feet like a recalcitrant four-year-old. "It all happened rather suddenly."

He looked around the room as if he could summon his brothers from thin air. Or, better yet, his surprise of a wife. But no one materialized, his brothers no doubt sharing a wee dram with Bea's husband Effric by now, and Ailis whisked away by Bea's sister to have a look at her head wound.

"Is the lass with child, then?" Bea asked, eyes narrowing as she crossed her arms over her ample bosom.

"God, no. I'd ne'er compromise a lady like that." He felt his ears growing warm and winced at her officious glare. "At least not and present her here to you."

"Well then, why the hurry?" Bealag Macqueen had never suffered fools lightly. She'd taken care of all three boys growing up, and as a cousin of sorts had remained part of their family even after they'd outgrown her.

"We've known each other for a while," he hedged. "It's only recently that we realized there was more to our...our relationship." Like shared animosity toward Ailis' brother and his men at arms. Manus Macaidie at the top of that list.

"Well, I canna say I'm sorry to see you choose a wife. I always feared that of the three of you, you'd be the one least likely to find the time to settle down. Always out there fighting others' battles."

Again Ranald felt a rush of guilt, only this time it was

well-founded. He'd been ordered to the king's guard. A royal decree. Not something to be ignored. But also not the life for a woman like Ailis.

"'Tis high time you thought of yourself and your own happiness," Bea was saying.

"I've lived life as I've chosen," Ranald protested. "Ye canna fault me for that."

"Nay. But 'tis far better to be loved than revered. You'll see. But enough of my bletherin'. Ye'll be anxious to join your bride. But afore you go, tell me why you brought Manus Macaide's men here."

Alarm crested at the tone in his old nurse's voice. "You know him, then?"

"I ken who he is. And what I know of him is no' good. 'Tis no' a man I'd turn my back on."

"I canna disagree with you there, but he's Ailis' kin and as such he's determined to protect her. Although I'd say there's definitely more to his tale. He claims Duncan Macintosh made him head of Ailis' clan, as well as promising him her hand in marriage."

"Well, you certainly put an end to those plans, I'd say. The chieftain is no' a fan of the Davidsons. And I canna believe he'd e'er choose the likes o' Macaidie over you. And besides, the deed is done."

He hated that he wasn't telling her the whole truth. But his loyalty had to lie with Ailis, and she'd not welcome his sharing her secrets. Not even with a woman he'd trust with his life.

"Aye. That it is," he replied, shaking his head to clear his thoughts. "And as her husband, I'll fight for her right to lead her clan."

"As you should. But all of that means Macaidie will see you as someone standing in the way of all that he wants. I guess we should count our blessings. He could have stayed here with his men."

"He claimed he wanted to ready Tur nan Clach for our arrival."

"More likely he's readying a trap o' some kind."

"You know that I trust your instincts, Bea. And we'll be careful. There's still the matter of the men who attacked Ailis. I don't know yet how Manus fits into the scheme, but until I do, I'll be keeping a close eye on him."

"Aye." She nodded, looking pleased. "You were always the canny one."

"I thought I was your favorite," Kendric said as he and Benneit strode into the solar.

"I dinna say Ranald was my favorite," she replied, eyes twinkling. "Just that he was the smartest."

Kendric cuffed Ranald on the shoulder as he walked by.

Benneit grinned at both of his brothers. "Well, we know that she always thought I was the handsomest."

"Come now. I've a fondness for you all—when you behave," she warned, her tone lacking anything but gentle amusement. "Now what have you done with my Effric, boys? Surely you're too old for toads in the boots?"

"You wound me, Bea," Benneit replied. "We've naught but love for Effric, and well you know it."

"You've naught but love for me, and still I had to endure your antics for all the years I took care of you three."

Benneit ducked his head, clearly embarrassed. Ranald was delighted that he wasn't the only one reduced to boyhood in the older woman's presence.

"Effric sent us to get you," Kendric said. "There's trouble in the kitchens, and apparently only you can make it right."

"Well, there's truth in that to be sure. The man has no' a diplomatic bone in his body." She grinned, the gesture making her look much younger. "I'll leave you to it, then." She waved at a collection of bottles set on a table by the fireplace, then turned to Ranald. "And should you be wondering, your wife is in the chamber directly above this one."

His wife. God's teeth, what in the world was he to do with a wife?

CHAPTER 7

*A*ilis sat on a bench and eased a comb through her tangled hair. Her hand moved with a soothing rhythm, but her eyes remained locked on the arched wooden door. Ranald's old nursemaid, Bea, had insisted on giving the newlyweds the best chamber in the tower. The thought gave her pause. *Newly-wed.* Hand-fasted. The idea seemed inconceivable. Impossible. And yet with one sentence she'd made it so. Compounded by Ranald's own acceptance and his brothers' witness, but still her doing. After everything she'd been through in life, she'd intended never to marry. Never to become the property of a man.

And yet here she sat, waiting for Ranald and wondering how in the world she was going to explain her impetuous act.

The door behind her opened and she swiveled, heart pounding, but it was only a servant.

"I beg your pardon if I'm interrupting, but Bea asked me to lay a fire. 'Tis best for you to stay warm after riding in the cold wind." The woman moved across to the stone fireplace to place some peat upon the grate. She was young. Maybe only a bit older than Ailis. Her fiery red hair was piled on her head, her dress made of finer material than that usually worn by a maidservant.

"I'm Ailis," she said, surprised that her voice sounded faint. Her head ached and in truth she just wanted to be alone—or with Ranald.

"Aye." The woman smiled. "I know. I'm Elspeth. I know your cousin, Marsle. Her mother and mine were great friends."

"I've not seen her for so long now. We try to stay in touch, but messages take time. Is she well?"

"That she is. Set to be married afore long, or so the gossip goes." Elspeth stirred the coals and the fire caught. "But here, I should be offering my felicitations not rambling on about your cousin."

Ailis swallowed and forced a smile. "Thank you. Ranald and I were wed yestereve." Or, in all truth, this nooning by the river. Guilt swamped through her, but she pushed it away; now wasn't the time. She lifted a hand to her cheek. "I'm afraid I'm still new to all of this."

"Ach, from what I've seen Ranald Macqueen is a fine man." Her smile widened, her expression teasing as she rose from beside the fire. "Any woman would be pleased to share his bed."

Elspeth's smile was contagious, or maybe Ailis was simply enjoying the idea of Ranald in her bed. Her cheeks flushed hotter, but her smile was genuine. "Which makes me truly honored that he chose me." Except, of course, that he hadn't.

"I wish you both well." Elspeth dusted her hands as she moved toward the door. "You're for Tur nan Clach on the morrow?"

"Aye, we are."

"Then tell Marsle I was asking about her."

"I will." Ailis nodded, holding her smile until the woman was gone, the door firmly shut.

With a sigh, she winced slightly as she pulled her hair back away from the gash. Bea's sister, Rhona, had tended the wound. Bathing it in a sweet smelling elixir and then applying a salve. It was still painful, but was no longer open and bleeding.

She'd set out from Moy with a hopeful heart and now... now she was examining her wounds and awaiting her husband while her worst enemy was at Tur nan Clach preparing God knows what for her arrival while his men sat downstairs drinking Bea's ale. Despite his posturing to the contrary, she had no doubt that Manus posed a threat. Both to her, and by association, to Ranald. The man had been trying to get his hands on her for as long as she could remember. It was only because of her brother's machinations that she had managed to avoid him.

At one time Alistair had believed he could convince Iain to marry Ailis. Only when that had proved a failure had he considered giving her to Manus. She shuddered, remembering just how close she'd come to being forced to marry the man. Ironically, it had been Iain—and Ranald—who had saved her from that fate, literally pulling her from her brother's dungeon.

And then her brother's death and her uncle's succession had thankfully lessened her value in Manus's eyes. But with her uncle gone, Manus had clearly seen his chance and appealed to the chieftain. Duncan Mackintosh had made it clear that he wanted Ailis to marry. And he needed to keep the Davidsons under control. It mattered little to him the kind of man Manus was. Or the hell to which he'd be banishing her.

In pledging herself to Ranald, Ailis had thwarted Manus's plan. In effect, she'd ripped the clan out from under him.

Although he could complain to the chieftain and perhaps still be awarded Tur nan Clach, there were blood ties between the Macqueens and the Macintoshes. And Ailis couldn't see Duncan choosing Manus over Ranald. The thought gave her comfort even as her stomach churned to think of the position she'd forced Ranald into. He was a warrior, not a laird. And he'd been summoned by the king.

'Twas his lifelong dream, and she'd snatched it from him as surely as she'd pledged her troth. Forced him into a life he had no desire for. Shackled him to a wife he'd not chosen. Her heart twisted and she turned away from her reflection, fighting tears. How could she possibly ever make this right?

"Ailis?"

She spun toward the door at the sound of Ranald's voice, her chest tightening with emotion. He looked so strong standing there in the archway. She fought against the urge to run to him. To beg him to hold her close so that she could lose herself in the comfort of his embrace. But she'd already asked too much of him. Instead, she forced a wan smile. "Your old nurse was very welcoming. She and her husband have both been so kind. And Rhona is almost as good as Katherine with herbs and remedies."

"Your head does not pain you o'er much, then?" He stepped into the chamber, his gaze moving across the bruises and gash.

"'Tis much better," she assured him, taking a step closer. "It only hurts a little. Rhona washed it with some concoction that seems to have stilled the pain."

"I'm glad." He lifted a hand as if to brush back her hair but let it fall again, clearly as uncomfortable as she.

"I…" They both started to speak at once then broke off, eyeing each other in strained silence.

"You first," Ranald finally said.

Ailis squared her shoulders. "I'm sorry to have dragged

you into all of this. I never should have insisted on going home so soon. If only I'd waited then…then—"

"Then you'd have found yourself bound to Manus Macaidie."

"But instead I've trapped you into marriage. God's truth, I don't know what came over me. It's just that Manus has always terrified me. I barely escaped him the first time. And the idea that Duncan had given him the right to…to…" She held up a pleading hand. "I have no excuse. I just…I just panicked. But surely we can find a way to make it right. To undo what I've done."

"Is that what you want, then? To be free of me?" His words were low and soft.

"No." She struggled to find the right words. "I mean, if there were any man I wished to belong to, it would be you. But neither of us truly wants to be wed. You've been called into service for the king. And I…I have a life at Tur nan Clach."

"Not if Manus Macadie has anything to say about it."

Terror washed through her at his pronouncement, her knees buckling, and blindly she reached out to find her balance. Strong arms encircled her, holding her steady.

"I didn't mean to scare you, lass. I'll no' let that bastard hurt a hair on your head."

"But I'm not your responsibility." Even as she said the words she knew that they were a lie. "At least I shouldn't be. If only I'd kept my mouth shut."

"You did what you had to do." This time he did brush the hair back from her face, his touch both soothing and exciting. "I canna fault you for that. And at least for the time being, until we can sort things out, I think we need to continue as we are."

"Married, you mean."

"Aye. 'Tis the best way of keeping you safe."

"But I can't ask you to make that kind of sacrifice for me."

"Mayhap, but 'tis already done."

She looked up at him, losing herself in the blue-green of his eyes. For a moment they breathed in tandem, hearts pounding the same rhythm, and then she pulled free, needing space to think.

"But what of the king?"

"We'll face that problem when the need arises. For now 'tis best to concentrate on the threat that Manus Macadie presents."

"His men are still downstairs?"

"Aye. Effric has offered them a place outside the walls to bed down. But they've insisted on being close to you."

She shuddered, crossing her arms as if to protect herself.

"Ailis, you have nothing to fear. I'll no' let them come anywhere near you. Or Manus either for that matter."

"You can't be with me all of the time. And Manus has always been one to take what he wants." Again she fought against a tremor of fear.

"Did he—" Ranald paused, sucking in a breath as his face tightened in anger. "Did he hurt you? Before. When he was your brother's captain?"

She stared at the floor, memories threatening to upend her hard-fought control. "Not in the way you mean. He hasn't...he didn't...he tried to force me once, but Alisdair walked in and put a stop to it. I was meant for Iain, you see. And he didn't want the goods harmed, so to speak."

"Your brother was a vile man, but in this instance I canna be displeased that he was there."

"Well, he wasn't so protective once Iain married Katherine. After that he...he locked me away and sent for Manus. I was to be his bride. A punishment for failing to win Iain."

"But we found you." She could tell from his expression

that he was remembering the dank hole they'd pulled her from.

"Yes, and rescued me from a fate worse than death. Manus Macaidie is an evil man. He takes what he wants and then destroys it." She lifted her gaze, recognizing that she'd pulled him once again into the horror that was her life. "I swear I didn't mean for you to be a part of all this. I wasn't thinking at all, really. I just wanted to stop Manus from believing he had any rights where I was concerned."

Again Ranald crossed the room and pulled her into his arms, his chin resting on the top of her head, his arms warm and strong as they surrounded her. "All will be well, I promise you. We'll work it out, but for now I think the best thing we can do is continue with this marriage. Let Macaidie and his men believe that you are under my protection. And that any move against you is a move against the Macqueens and, by blood-ties, against Chattan. I've already sent word to Duncan, and I'll send a missive to the king at first light."

"But that will only bind us more tightly together." She pulled back so that she could see him.

"That it shall. But in so doing, we keep you safe. And for the moment, that's all that matters. Come now. You need rest. Tomorrow we head for Tur nan Clach."

The thought of going home should have made her happy, but instead it only heightened her guilt. She'd let her desire to make things right with her clan overrule all rational thought. Men were trying to kill her, and still she'd insisted on leaving the safety of Duncreag. And she'd practically forced Ranald to come along for the ride. He was nothing if not gallant.

With his arm around her waist he drew her toward the bed. "I'll give you some time to get ready, and then I'll be back."

She jerked out of her tumbling thoughts, her gaze

colliding with his as hot color washed across her face. "You're sleeping here?"

"Aye. You know as well as I that in order to give full credence to the words we spoke, there has to be a consummation."

Ailis's breath caught in her throat.

"Dinna fash yourself, lass. All we have to do is make it seem as if we're sharing a bed. In truth, I can sleep on the floor. 'Tis important to keep up appearances for Bea and Effric. Not to mention Manus' men. Besides, there's no way I'm leaving you on your own. Not with Manus' guard out there."

She wanted to protest. To tell him that he didn't have to take it this far. But she couldn't find the words, instead taking solace in the fact that he was going to stay and see this thing through—that no matter what came of their marriage, in the end, he would make certain that she was kept safe. It wasn't fair to him and that fact alone should give her pause. But all she felt in the moment was relief, and, if she were completely honest, a rush of something that felt dangerously close to love.

❧

*R*anald strode down the corridor leading to the great hall, in search of his brothers. There was no question that things had gotten out of control. And yet he couldn't shake the sense that somehow, in truth, all was as it should be. With the exception of course of Manus Macaidie. The man was a threat to Ailis. And Ranald was determined to keep her safe.

He told himself he'd do as much for anyone. Particularly a friend of Katherine and Iain's. But if he were being honest, he knew that it was more than just that. From the first time he'd met her, there'd been something about Ailis that called to him. He could still see her curled up on a window seat at Duncreag, listening as he'd shared tales of his and Iain's adventures.

The warmth of her smile and the sweet sound of her laughter had filled the places in his heart he hadn't known existed. And then later, when he'd realized her brother's treachery and they'd found Ailis a captive in the dungeons at Tur nan Clach, his rage had been far deeper than just the anger caused by the threat to Katherine. He'd wanted to kill Alisdair Davidson himself.

But afterward, the timing for the two of them had been wrong. Their conversations had been awkward, Ailis blaming herself for her brother's sins and Ranald needing distance from his cousin and his newly found happiness. Iain and Ranald had always been of the same mind. Fighting and wenching with the best of them. But suddenly Ranald saw Iain in a different light. Katherine made him different.

Better.

And Ranald had felt too much the voyeur, watching the two of them in their joy. He loved them both dearly, but he'd departed with a sigh of relief and the determination to find a good fight to clear his head. And he'd done just that, battling with his brothers for his father and the Macqueens.

But something inside him had changed as well. Something that he couldn't or wouldn't put a name to. Something softer. Something needy. Something beyond anything he'd ever felt before. And he'd hated what he'd perceived as a weakness. Despised it, in all truth. But mayhap he'd been wrong.

Here, now, knowing that Ailis was in the chamber above and that she needed him—that she possibly even wanted him —he felt suddenly as if he'd found his place. As barmy as the notion seemed, perhaps he needed her, too.

He shook his head, pushing the thought away. He needed no one. Never had. Never would. He cared for the lass. She was a part of his extended family. And she required protection. *His* protection. It was the least he could do.

The rest of it—well, as he'd told her, they'd deal with it after she was safe. Then she could go her way and he could go his.

The thought should have soothed him. But instead his stomach roiled and he clenched a fist as he walked into the great room. He stopped first for a word with Fergus and William and then strode over to the dais where his brothers sat.

"Ah, the prodigal returns," Kendric said, handing Ranald a tankard of ale.

"I've only been gone a short time, you eejit. That hardly bears celebrating my return."

"Mayhap," Benneit said, "But when that time is spent in the company o' someone as bonny as Ailis, 'tis a moment worth celebrating by my reckoning. Especially considering you've only just married the lass."

"You know well enough that 'tis no' a regular marriage," Ranald snapped, draining the cup Kendric had given him.

"Stop your blethering," Kendric said, eyes flashing a warning as he tipped his head toward a table in the far corner of the hall.

Ranald clamped his mouth shut, angry at his own carelessness. Macaidie's men sat drinking before the fire. Far enough away that he was fairly sure they hadn't heard his comments, but close enough for Ranald to feel the fool. He'd not protect Ailis if he let his mouth have free rein.

Talking ceased as a pretty redheaded lass set a tray of ale before them, their eyes collectively moving to her breasts. She leaned closer to the biggest bruiser and whispered something. The man nodded and then grinned as she sashayed away with a wink and smile.

"You'd think they were honored guests by the rate they're drinking Bealag and Effric's ale." Benneit tilted a head in their direction as he filled Ranald's cup from a pitcher on the table, lowering his voice. "I meant no insult by talk of Ailis, brother. And while I know 'tis all a fine tangle, I canna help but wonder if maybe the two of you belong together somehow. Maybe this was all fated."

"Since when have you believed in that sort of rot?" Ranald growled, not certain where his anger was coming from.

"I dinna pretend to believe anything. I only mean that when you and Ailis are together, there's something more than just the two of you. Something bigger." He waved his hand through the air, clearly having problems with his words.

"I've no idea what the hell you're talking about." Ranald grimaced as he sipped the ale.

"In truth, neither have I." Benneit laughed, and Ranald's tension eased. Despite their differences, he knew that his brothers would die for him. No questions asked.

"So what are you going to do?" Kendric's voice, like Benneit's, was carefully modulated.

"About my wife?" he asked, shooting a look in the direction of the men flanking the fireplace. "I intend to deliver her safely to Tur nan Clach. And stay until I know that she's truly out of harm's way."

"Meaning Manus Macaidie is taken care of." Kendric's words were not a question.

"Aye. Did you send the messenger to Duncan?"

"I did," Kendric assured him. "I sent Ewen and told him to make all possible haste. We should hear something soon after we arrive at Tur nan Clach."

"What of the king?" Benneit asked. "What will you tell him?"

"The truth. That I've taken a wife and that I'll need to settle things with her before I can come to him."

"You realize that you're only tightening that which binds the two of you. With both the king and Chattan aware of your situation, there'll be no easy way to separate."

"I'm well aware," he sighed. "But I canna leave her on her own. Not now. Not with Macaidie and his men ready to pounce at the first sign of weakness. For the moment we hold the upper hand. But I've no idea what we'll face when we reach her holding."

"Then perhaps we shouldn't go. We can turn about and return to Duncreag. Ailis will be safe with Iain. He's got the men to protect her. And the power of Chattan behind him."

"We've got the same protection. From both Iain and Chattan. I canna believe that Macaidie would dare to openly thwart the chieftain. He's far more likely to bide his time. And wait for an opportunity. We've just got to make certain that he never gets one."

""Twould be easier if we were to take him out of contention."

"Aye, but we canna act against him until we're at Tur nan Clach. And even then we'll need to be careful. There are no doubt others who support him. Not to mention his agreement with the Chief. I canna believe that Duncan would side with Macaidie over me, but I also dinna want to take the chance of angering him until I understand better where he stands."

"You'd turn Ailis over to Duncan if he tells you to?"

"Nay. She's mine." The words came almost of their own accord, but he'd not deny them. "I'll no' let Manus Macaidie, or any man, lay a finger on her. But if Duncan insisted, I'd take her away from Tur nan Clach."

"She'd never forgive you," Kendric observed.

"Aye, but she'd be alive and safe and far away from Manus Macaidie. Sometimes what's best isn't what you want. And I canna let her throw her life away for a wee piece of land."

"'Tis more than that, and well you know it."

"That I do. But I will no' let anyone hurt her, including Duncan. And if that means taking her away, then so be it."

"There's wisdom in your words," Benneit said, fingering the dirk at his side, "but still that does no' mean that I wouldn't love to make that bastard Manus pay for everything he's done to your Ailis."

"You and me both, brother." Ranald swallowed the bitter ale, his gut tightening as he saw again the fear that washed across Ailis' face when Macaidie stepped into that clearing. He'd also witnessed her strength as she'd rallied and stood her ground. Pride filled his heart. Pride and something warmer—deeper. God's teeth, if he wasn't careful, he was in danger of falling for his wee wife and her courageous ways.

CHAPTER 8

*A*ilis opened her eyes, sleep clouding her brain. She struggled for cognizant thought, pushing the haze aside as she reached for the dirk under her pillow. Something wasn't right.

Her heart pounded as her muscles tensed and she listened for a repeat of the sound that had jerked her from sleep. Memories of the past invaded, coloring the present with terrors of nights long gone. Something moved. Her breath stuttered.

The embers of the fire did little to illuminate the room and the fur hanging over the narrow window blocked out any moonlight. Shadows shifted as she strained to see something in the dark.

The door rattled slightly as it slowly slid open.

Grasping the dirk Katherine had given her by the handle Ailis pushed off the bed, holding her breath, her mind still trying to separate nightmare from reality. A sliver of light sliced across the room.

She froze for a moment, then silently glided across the floor.

As the door slid open she moved behind it, clutching the little knife, waiting, her breath coming in ragged gasps.

The dark figure of a man filled the doorway and she lurched forward, arm raised. "One more inch and I'll skin you alive." Her hand trembled, but thankfully her voice held steady.

"Ach, but lass, surely you're no' already planning to do away with your husband." The sound of his voice rumbled through her and she lowered her arm, relief and regret rushing through her.

"Ranald." The dirk dropped to the floor, clattering against the wooden planks. "I thought...I thought..." Tears filled her eyes as her terror faded.

His strong arms closed around her. "I'm here, Ailis. There's no need for fear. Manus is far away and his men are no threat. My brothers are outside the door, even now watching o'er us. Between their swords and mine," he said, patting the claymore by his side, "there's nothing for you to fear. I swear it on my life."

She gulped a breath and pressed closer, embarrassed by her own fears. "Manus is dangerous. I would be lying if I said otherwise. I canna believe I've pulled you into the pain that is my life. It isn't fair. I've been nothing but selfish." She pulled back, her gaze meeting his, her stomach clenching as she faced the hard truth of what she'd done.

In linking her life with his, she'd pulled him into the hell her brother had wrought. The terror he and Manus had inflicted not only on her but on her entire clan. And despite the fact that she hated her own weakness, she relished the fact that for this moment at least she was no longer alone.

"I make my own choices, Ailis. Never doubt that." His words were muffled as he pulled her close again, but they resonated through his chest as she pressed against him, needing his strength as much as a breath or heartbeat.

"But I forced your hand," she whispered.

"No one has ever forced me to do anything." He stroked her hair, his touch soothing and disturbing all at the same time. "Come. Let's get you settled into bed. We've a hard ride ahead of us tomorrow, and there's no telling what faces us when we reach the end of our journey. You need sleep."

"Only if you stay here." She glanced over at the rumpled covers. "With me." The words sounded so needy. And yet she didn't want to lose the strength of his arms. It was somehow as if his holding her made her stronger. Made her whole.

"As you wish," he replied, his voice deep and soothing.

"When I'm in your arms I feel complete in a way I canna even explain. Or pretend that I understand."

He paused for a moment and she tensed, thinking she'd gone too far. Asked too much. This man who had come back into her life and been swept up in the turmoil that had always surrounded her. In a moment of panic she'd tied her life to his without so much as asking his blessing. And now their lives were intertwined in a way that she wanted so badly, yet knew was unfair.

"Come lass. Tomorrow will bring new challenges and we'll face them together. But for now, rest. Just let me hold you."

He helped her onto the bed, and after divesting himself of his sword and plaid, joined her. Pulling her into his arms he settled them both under the linen and furs, making a nest for the two of them.

"But I," she started, not really sure what she wanted to say; only certain that she didn't want him to leave her. Ever.

"Hush now. Sleep." His warm breath whispered against her temple, her body relaxing as she settled into his warmth. In truth, she wanted to kiss him again. To feel his body move against hers. But there was so much between them. So much that she had to consider. Her future. *His* future. It was all too much. And with a little sigh, she let go, knowing deep inside that as long as he held her in his arms nothing could harm her.

Between Ranald and his brothers, she was safe. Truly safe. And while she knew in the end she had to fight her own battle, she also recognized that this man was everything she'd ever wanted. Everything she'd ever dreamed of. And the idea made her heart swell with both joy and terror.

His arms tightened around her. For a moment she let the idea of safety and sleep surround her, and then she fought against the easy way out. She wanted this man. Wanted him like no other. For many months, if she were honest. Ranald represented all that she believed life was supposed to be. Love. Trust. Honor. Everything.

She lifted her face to his, heart pounding.

For a moment he looked at her, as if trying to solve a puzzle, the firelight playing across his face. And then his lips met hers, first in a gentle exploratory kiss, and then with the hard possessiveness of a man who knew what he wanted. It should have frightened her. Lord knew she'd fought off advances before. But this was different. Along with the power of his kiss there was a question.

A desire to know if she wanted what he offered. With a sigh of pure release, she opened her mouth to his, acquiescing to his touch—his demand. Her body tightened with desire. A heat she'd never experienced before. This man—his hands, his fingers, his lips—was beyond anything she'd ever imagined. His kiss robbed her of rational thought. How was it that his touch could be so blinding?

"Are ye sure, lass?" he asked, his voice caressing as his hands ran down the length of her arms.

"Yes." She nodded, her voice whisper-soft. "We've agreed to see this through. And so we have the right to... to see that…" She fumbled to a stop, heat spreading across her cheeks and chest.

"Aye," he said with a crooked smile. "We have the right. But more important is the pleasure it can bring. If that is what you wish, I am more than happy to oblige."

"I wish it very much." She ran her fingers down the hard length of his cheek and chin, the stubble of his night beard rough against her skin.

With a whispered sigh she closed the distance between them, tipping her head back, offering herself to him.

Ranald bent his head and brushed his lips against hers. She moaned and pressed closer, their passion echoing in the movements of their lips. This was the way it was supposed to be.

She explored the planes of his shoulders, massaging little circles, the feel of his skin igniting a fire deep inside her. He stroked the line of her back, his hand moving lower, cupping her bottom, pulling her tightly against him. They surged together, fitting as if two halves of a whole.

Still locked in the kiss, Ranald slid a hand up to cup her breast. Sparks shot through her as he circled the nipple with his thumb.

"Ach lass, you feel so bonny. Are you sure?" He whispered the words against her lips and she nodded, breaking away enough so that her gaze could meet his.

"I want you, Ranald. Only you." Her lips were moist, her eyes dark with passion.

He searched her face for a minute more, and then with a groan of satisfaction, pulled her back into his arms, his mouth closing over hers. She sighed, opening her mouth to him, offering her trust as their tongues tangled together, circling, caressing. Taking and giving. It was as if they'd done this a million times before. She knew his smell, his taste. Everything about him was intimately familiar. And yet this was uncharted territory, her need and his twining together into something more powerful than just hunger or desire.

She ached inside. Not just from wanting him but from needing him. His hands spanned her waist as he pulled her closer. His mouth moved from her lips, raining kisses along her cheeks and jaw. He pulled her earlobe between his teeth, sucking lightly as heat pooled in her belly.

Then he dipped his head, his tongue following the smooth curve of her neck, pausing to caress the hollow at its base where her pulse pounded. His hands rose to her back, holding her as his mouth plundered. Sucking and licking until she squirmed with need.

With a muttered oath he reached for the hem of her night shift and pulled it over her head, tossing it beside the bed. Still holding her with one hand, he bent her back and his lips closed around one bare breast, his tongue circling her nipple, his heated touch sending shivers coursing through her. He teased the nipple, biting gently, and then pulled it into his mouth, sucking deeply.

Ailis clenched, sensation threatening to overwhelm her.

From one breast he moved to the other, and then lifted her again so that his lips crushed down on hers. The hunger between them stretched tight, and Ailis found it impossible to breathe. Never in her life had she felt this kind of heat—this kind of power. It surged through her—through them—as the kiss deepened, their passion threatening to consume them.

She slid her hands beneath his tunic, moving across the rock-hard muscles of his abdomen and the velvety smoothness of his chest. She was entranced by his strength. His masculinity.

Her desire reaching a fever pitch, she pushed his shirt higher and he raised his arms, breaking their kiss as she pulled it over his head. Shivering with need, she swallowed and then he was there—holding her, his mouth closing over hers, taking possession of not just the kiss but of her. For a moment she trembled, guilt and shame threatening as she remembered the past.

But then Ranald's arms tightened around her. "Easy lass, 'tis only the two of us."

She sighed, feeling safe. Protected. Loved. Somewhere deep inside her mind protested the validity of the last thought. But then he was kissing her again and she pressed against him, her breasts tight against his chest. His hands slid down the smooth skin of her back, then lower still to cup her bottom, fingers kneading as he deepened his kiss. His touch was powerful and possessive. And Ailis arched against him, wanting more—wanting him.

Their tongues danced together as his hands slipped lower, caressing first the backs of her thighs, and then higher still. She shuddered in anticipation as his hand slipped between her legs, brushing across the sensitive skin of her inner thighs.

He kissed her breasts and then moved his mouth along the line of her belly. His fingers parted the curls between her legs, stoking her with his fingers. She sucked in a breath as a tingling sensation washed through her.

"Come now, lass," he whispered. "Let me love you." She clung to the sound of his voice and feel of his hands as he knelt before her, pushing her thighs apart. And then with a wicked grin he dipped his head and kissed her soft, swelling heat. Ailis's breath caught in her throat, as he pushed her wider still, his tongue probing, circling, caressing, and stroking until she tangled her hands in his hair, urging him onward.

The heat rose inside her, intensity building until she was quivering with her need. And still he licked and stroked her, his tongue finding the tender nub and pulling it into his mouth. Ailis jerked with the contact, her body tightening as passion ratcheted higher. Sucking now, he slipped one strong finger inside her, gently moving it in and out—the motion finding rhythm with the ministrations of his tongue.

Teetering at the edge, she clutched his head, as if in so doing she'd found an anchor. But then his fingers, two of them now, thrust hard and deep, his mouth moving over her. Laving. Loving.

Ailis arched as she flew apart, sensation banishing all cognizant thought. Moving up to sit beside her, he gathered her close, his breath stirring her hair as she struggled to regain her breath. For a moment she lay against him, boneless, her body still shuddering in the aftermath. He stroked her breasts, her shoulders, her hair, and then he was kissing her again, his hands moving across her body. Touching her everywhere. Stroking. Caressing. Tormenting her.

Ailis felt her need rising once more. And she slid her fingers down the hard length of his chest, across the ridges of his abdomen, and then lower still until her fingers circled his velvet heat.

Ranald sighed as she closed her fingers around him, and slowly—so slowly—began to stroke. Up and down, tightening her hand then releasing it, only to tighten it once again, savoring his strength, his power. His fingers tangled through her hair, his body bowing upward as she continued to stroke him.

With an audible groan, Ranald pulled her back up to his mouth. "Enough, *mo ghràdh*," he whispered. "I need to be inside you. Now."

Ailis nodded, her own body thrumming with the thought. She'd never known it could be like this. So powerful. So consuming. She swallowed as he rolled her beneath him, pushing apart her thighs, his hardness pressed against her opening. And then with one slow thrust he was inside her.

"Am I hurting you, lass?" he whispered.

"Nay." Ailis shook her head, marveling at the rightness of it. The way he filled her. Completed her. For a moment they held still, gazes colliding as they both absorbed the enormity of what was happening. And then he began to move. She tilted her hips, taking him deeper, finding his rhythm and moving with him.

Stronger and deeper. Faster and harder. Until Ailis was no longer certain where she left off and he began. His mouth found hers and their tongues moved together, mimicking the rhythm of their bodies. His hands cupped her hips, lifting her higher, and she wrapped her legs around him, taking him deeper still.

Body to body. Soul to soul.

Moving together until she shattered, convulsing around him as he, too, found his pleasure. As she drifted slowly back to the soft warmth of the bed, there was no doubt in her mind that tomorrow there would be a price to pay. But tonight—tonight she belonged to Ranald. And at least for this one moment—he belonged to her, too.

CHAPTER 9

"*A*ilis, *mo ghràdh*, I need you to awaken." Ranald caressed Ailis' cheek, and she sighed with pleasure as she slowly opened her eyes. His hair was tousled and his eyes full of an emotion she wasn't sure she could name. With a smile she reached for him, but he shook his head, his fingers still gently cupping her face.

"Ach, lass, as much as I've a need to love you again, I canna. Kendric says there's trouble at the gate."

She sat up, pushing back her hair, her eyes darkening with concern.

"Dinna fash yourself. We've more than enough men to handle anything Manus throws at us. But I dinna want you to wake and find yourself alone." He grabbed his plaid and deftly wrapped it around his torso.

"Do you think he's come back?" Ailis asked, rising to help him pin the Macqueen badge into place.

"I canna say, but even if he has, my brothers and I will protect you."

"I'm not worried about myself. It's you I worry about. If

anything happened..." she trailed off, her eyes wide and beseeching.

"Nothing is going to happen, *leannan*. I canna even say if the threat is real. Just that Benneit and Kendric asked me to come. I promise everything will be fine." He leaned down to kiss her forehead, but she tipped her head up so that their lips met. For a moment sweetness reigned, and then as if by silent agreement, it deepened into something more. A promise—a covenant.

"You'll send word if you've need of me?" she asked as they pulled apart.

"Aye." He took his claymore from beside the bed. "And also if I think there's need for you to move to safer ground."

"Leave the holding, you mean?"

"'Tis possible, but more likely a move to the tower's cellars or somewhere with limited access. Bea or the other women here will know the best place to go if needed. Just promise you'll do what is asked if the time comes."

"Of course. I will always heed your words. But I cannot promise that I'll leave if I believe that you're in danger." She ran her hands across his chest, smoothing his plaid while relishing his strength and heat. "I am your wife in truth now, and you are mine to protect just as much as I am yours."

"I ken. But I promise, between my brothers and Iain's men, all will be well." He kissed her again, the touch hard and possessive. "I'll be back before you know it."

As the door closed behind him Ailis sank back onto the bed, her heart pounding, worry clouding the joy that had been their joining. For a moment she'd allowed herself to forget the threat of her past. As long as Manus Macadie was alive, she could never rest easy. Even with Ranald and his brothers in her corner she wasn't truly safe, nor were the people in her clan.

She was putting innocent people in danger just being

here at Bea's holding. And she'd meant what she said: Ranald and the people he cared about were hers to protect. Moving quickly, she donned her shift and overdress, tying a simple silver cord at her waist.

Using a brush and ribbon, she quickly braided and secured her long hair. Throwing it over her shoulder, she took a deep breath and crossed to the door, ready to face whatever challenges lay ahead.

The corridor outside her chamber was empty, flickering candlelight from the torches on the wall dancing with the shadows. She took a step in the direction of the solar but then changed her mind, heading instead for the other side of the tower to the chamber where Bea's sister Rhona had attended Ailis' wounds. From there she should at least be able to gain a glimpse of the front gate at the bottom of the open courtyard.

The hallway was quiet, eerily so, most of the tower's inhabitants no doubt still abed. She shivered as she rounded a corner and climbed a set of spiral stairs to the next level. The keeping chamber door was ajar, but Ailis knocked anyway. When there was no answer she pushed the door open and stepped inside. Fortunately, the remnants of a fire still burned on the grate, providing enough light for her to see that the room was empty. Sighing, she moved to the narrow window, not certain if she were relieved or concerned to be alone.

Beyond the tower's walls, Ailis could see the glimmer of torchlight. Proof then that something was afoot. She searched among the crowd of men below, looking for something to indicate her husband's location. He and his brothers were taller than most of the men, but it was simply too far and too dark for her to be certain.

Turning from the window she sent a prayer heavenward, asking for protection for Ranald and his brothers. Perhaps this was all nothing more than a misunderstanding. Manus' men moving out. Or perhaps settling in for the night. Even as she had the thought, she heard yelling in the distance and shivered, her head telling her that something was most definitely wrong.

Squaring her shoulders, she crossed the room back into the hall, determined to find Bea or her sister. Together they would be strong while their men fought Manus'. She walked back the way she had come, and started down the stairs, only to hear someone call her name. Turning back, she recognized Elspeth pulling a plaid around her shoulders as she hurried forward.

"Thank goodness I've found ye," the woman said. "When I saw you were gone from yer bedchamber, I feared the worst."

"I'm fine," Ailis assured her. "Just trying to find Bea or Rhona."

"They've gone to the cellars. 'Tis safer there."

"Then we must join them." Ailis started again for the stairs, but Elspeth reached out to stop her with a hand to her shoulder.

"Nay. We're to go to the tunnels," Elspeth said. "Ranald is going to meet you at the end and take you to safety while the others hold the bastards back."

"Are they attacking, then?" Ailis asked, fear for Ranald making her throat tighten.

"I dinna know. But if they haven't they will, mark my words. Manus Macaidie is no' the kind of man to let go of something he believes is his."

"And by something you mean me."

"Aye, that I do. But come now, we must go afore we canna get out safely."

"But my husband—" Ailis began only to be cut off with a wave of Elspeth's hand.

"Your man is the one who told me to come for you. I tell

you he and his brothers have a plan. And he'll no' be thanking you for wasted time blethering."

Ailis nodded and Elspeth grabbed her elbow, hurrying her along as they turned back down the corridor, passing the keeping room and taking a narrow staircase at the back of the tower. The stairs spiraled downward into the dark, and Ailis hesitated as Elspeth took the candle she was holding and lit a larger torch from its bracket on the wall. "That should be enough to light our way," she said, extinguishing the taper and starting down the stairs.

Ailis sucked in a breath and followed in Elspeth's wake, the narrow stairs twisting down, down and down again until she felt as if they were in the very bowels of the tower. Finally, there was a small landing and an arch that led into a cavernous chamber with an arched ceiling.

"Where are we?" she asked, moving closer to the circle of light being cast by the torch.

"'Tis the place where the tower's stores are kept. There's a tunnel here that links to a meadow some distance away. 'Tis easier to get things in and out, ye ken. And it provides a way out in times such as these when there's a need. Yer man will be meeting us in the meadow."

Elspeth moved toward a stack of boxes and then stepped behind them, calling out for Ailis to follow. For a moment she hesitated then remembered her promise to heed Ranald's words. "Right behind you," she replied, wishing that it were a little less dark and that the tunnel wasn't so damp and narrow. There was a similar room in Tur nan Clach, the place she'd been held captive; locked in a large iron cage after defying her brother.

In truth, she was still afraid of the dark.

But it had been Ranald who had rescued her then, and Ranald who was trying to save her now. So she held up her skirts and followed Elspeth into the narrow corridor. The ceiling was only just above her head, and water dripped in places as it saturated the roughly hewn walls. The stones beneath her feet were slick, too, with moisture. And she kept a hand to the wall to give her stability. Elspeth, too, was moving cautiously was they wound their way along the passageway, deeper into the dark.

"You're certain this is the right way?" Ailis asked, trying to quell the tremor in her voice.

"Aye, I know 'tis damp and cold, but 'tis only a wee bit further," Elspeth promised, moving a little faster as they rounded a bend—darkness still looming.

Elspeth held up the torch, the light illuminating two separate passageways. "You stay here while I check to be sure this is the right way," she said, already striding off in to the corridor, the light fading as she moved away, darkness overtaking Ailis.

She took a step to follow Elspeth, and then forced herself to stop. She was being foolish. The woman would be back. Still, the darkness felt like a living thing pulsing around her. Memories of the days spent in the dank, dark cage clawed at her now. She closed her eyes and forced herself to think of Ranald. Of his hands as they moved over her skin. Of his lips as they had caressed her breasts and body.

She could almost feel him there with her. Holding the dark at bay. Keeping her safe from harm. Her breathing slowed, her heart no longer pounding. Alisdair was dead and Ranald would find a way to stop Manus. Everything was going to be fine. She simply had to fight the fear and keep faith in her husband.

"'Tis this way," Elspeth's voice broke into Ailis's reverie and she opened her eyes, blinking in the light as the other woman pointed to the left corridor. "Not much further now."

Ailis nodded and gave Elspeth a shy smile. "Thank you for helping me. I canna tell you how much it means."

"'Tis of no import. I only wish to see ye safely away from the tower." She started down the tunnel, Ailis following close behind. It was drier here, with less of the slick moisture coating the walls and floor.

Ailis breathed easier when the darkness began to lighten slightly, a soft glow in the distance indicating that they were almost to the meadow.

"Will you be coming with us?" Ailis asked.

"Nay." Elspeth shook her head, her hand tightening on the torch. "I'm afraid your path and mine are very different."

Ailis frowned, something in the other woman's words setting off a frission of concern. "I'm afraid I don't understand," she said.

"Dinna fash yourself," Elspeth replied, casting an unreadable look over her shoulder. "We each have our purpose in this life. And mine is no' the same as yours."

Her words didn't help to soothe her worry, but she forced herself to smile. "Nevertheless, I am grateful for all that you've done." They reached a large boulder outlined with light. And for a moment, Ailis thought there'd been a mistake. "The way is blocked."

Elspeth smiled, the gesture not quite reaching her eyes. "Nay, ye just have to step around it. See, there's wee bit of space just here." She snuffed the torch and then stepped around the rock, disappearing behind it.

Ailis heaved a sigh of relief and moved forward to follow Elspeth, slipping through an opening that was much larger than it appeared from the other side. At first as she stepped into the meadow she blinked, adjusting to the light. Morning had come while they were making their way through the tunnels, the pink and orange rays reaching up into the sky just above the horizon.

Elspeth stood at the head of a horse, the rider cast in shadow by the rising sun. Ailis rushed forward, joy singing through her veins, but jerked to a halt as her vision cleared and the identity of the rider became certain.

"Ah Elspeth, I see you have succeeded in spiriting away my prize." Manus Macadie swung down from his horse and held out a hand. "Come, Ailis. Surely now I've proven to you that I never give up what is mine."

~

"I canna see the point of their waiting until full light," Kendric said as the three brothers stood in the shadows beyond the walls of the tower. "'Tis possible they've no intention of attacking."

"Aye," Benneit said, squinting as he looked into the first orange rays of sunrise. "They certainly are no' worried about us knowing they're out there."

"Still, we canna assume they'll no' come for us." Fergus waved his hand toward the camp. "I sent scouts and they reported an increase in numbers. Enough to, at the very least, trap us here until help arrives."

Ranald gripped the stone wall in front of him. "Did you manage to send a message to Duncreag?"

"I did." Fergus crossed his arms, turning to face the three of them. "I sent young Robbie. Which means Iain will be here soon enough. I say we ride out now and confront them. Call their bluff."

"I canna argue with your thinking. Force the battle on our terms instead of theirs," Benneit said.

"Except that none of this makes any sense." Ranald shook his head. "Why would Manus want to attack us here? We're fortified, and he has to know that we've called for reinforcements."

"Even if he wins there's no' guarantee he'll obtain anything of value," Benneit added.

"Mayhap the man is just barmy," Fergus shrugged.

"Or maybe this is a trap. An attempt to draw us away from the prize," Kendric said, his somber gaze meeting Ranald's.

"Ailis," Ranald breathed his wife's name and felt rage engulf him, his hands tightening into fists. "I'd die before I'd let that bastard touch her."

"Which may be precisely the point," Benneit said. "With you dead Ailis is free to marry elsewhere, and Duncan has already decreed that her husband be Manus..." He trailed off with an apologetic shrug.

"Well, that canna happen. I won't allow anyone to hurt my wife."

"Nor will we," Kendric was quick to reassure him.

"I'm still for attacking," Fergus growled, his hand on his claymore.

"Ranald."

They all turned at the sound of William's voice. He stood in the archway that connected the gate tower to the ramparts, the shadows hiding his face.

"*God's teeth*. What are you doing here? I told you to watch over Ailis."

"I was doing just that when Elspeth came and then took her to the cellars."

"Who the hell is Elspeth?" Benneit asked.

"She's one of the maidservants. The comely redhead," Kendric replied.

William stepped into the light, his face creased with worry. "I thought that mayhap Ailis had gone to be with Bea and her sister. They're sheltered in one of the fortified rooms below with the other women."

"And?" Ranald demanded with a wave of his hand, his heart-pounding.

"I still was no' certain that there was need to fret, because the tower is secure. We have all the exits guarded. I checked to be certain. And then I went to see for myself. Ailis is no' there. Bea and the others had no' seen her. And Elspeth has disappeared as well."

"They canna have gone far," Kendric said, his hand on Ranald's shoulder. "The lad said the exits were still secure."

"But that's the problem," William choked out, his face red with anger and worry. "There's another way out. One we dinna know of. Bea never thought of it. There's a tunnel used primarily for traders and such." William sucked in a breath. "I think they've taken Ailis."

CHAPTER 10

*A*ilis opened her mouth to scream, but nothing came out.

Elspeth took a step closer to Manus. "But you promised you were going to kill her. 'Tis me that you love."

"I dinna ken why you would think that." Manus' dark features shifted into a sneer. "Surely no' just because ye opened yer legs for me, ye stupid whore."

"Nay. Ye canna mean that," Elspeth said, her gaze locked on Manus. "We belong together. You said so yourself."

"I said what I needed to say to get ye to do my bidding. Mayhap if she'd died the first time, things could have been different." He shrugged her off, taking a step toward Ailis as she stood frozen, her nightmares coalescing into a frightening reality.

"'Twasn't my fault that the men you hired failed. I did as you told me. I manipulated Marsle and gave the information to you. And then I paid the men for you and set the plan in motion. Just as expected, they intercepted her near the abbey."

"But they dinna kill her. 'Tis as simple as that. And even if they had, truth is I'd already tired of you. Always underfoot, simpering and begging." He hit her then, and Elspeth stumbled backward.

Ailis instinctively reached out to keep her from falling. The other woman whirled on her, her face a mask of rage. "I'll no' let you steal my man." Her fingers closed like talons around Ailis' wrist, a knife blade glittering as she lifted her other arm.

Ailis tried to pull free of her clutching grasp but Elspeth held firm, the knife descending. Twisting to avoid the thrust Ailis turned, dipping her head, still struggling for freedom. The moments seemed to stretch endlessly as she awaited the blow, but instead she heard a hiss and felt Elspeth's full weight as she fell, Manus' sword buried deep in her side.

Bile rising, Ailis jerked her wrist free of the dead woman. Blood oozed from her mouth, her open eyes staring up at the sky. Manus cursed and pulled his blade from the body, turning his attention to Ailis. "Ye'll no' get away from me again. There's nowhere to run."

"My husband will find you," Ailis said as she frantically searched the clearing for a way to freedom.

"Yer husband is dead. My men will have seen to that."

"In the same way that Elspeth and your men supposedly saw to my demise?"

His mouth twisted into what passed for a grin and Ailis shuddered. "Believe me when I tell you, he's dead." Manus stepped forward, Elspeth's body still between them.

Ailis fought against the grief that threatened to swamp her and instead squared her shoulders, taking a careful step back. "Even if he's gone, I'll ne'er belong to you."

"You were promised to me by your brother, just as your father promised me Tur nan Clach." He took another step forward, his eyes lighting with anticipation. "You belong to me."

Grabbing her skirts with both hands, she turned and ran for the entrance of the tunnel. She could hear Manus behind her as he stumbled over Elspeth's body. Keeping her focus on the cleft in the rocks she forced herself to move faster, heart pounding as she slid into the darkness of the tunnel.

For a moment she was disoriented but she kept moving forward, her hand on the wall to guide her as she continued to run. Manus cried out in anger, and she knew she only had minutes to widen the gap between them. He was a warrior, but she was younger and more lithe. And he, too, was blinded by the dark. There was safety in the tower. Others who would protect her.

She just had to get there before Manus got to her.

The wall beneath her hand curved to the right and she bent to pick up a stone from the floor. As she continued to move forward she threw out her left hand, and as expected, felt an opening. The turn she'd seen earlier. Without stopping she threw the stone into the other corridor, and it skittered and tumbled into the darkness. She heard Manus slow behind her as he approached the opening.

Racing forward she ran on, her soft slippers making no further sound. She struggled to draw breath, her heart threatening to break free of her chest but still she ran. And then suddenly ahead she saw a faint light. It was too soon to be the doorway to the cellars, but she felt a wash of joy and pushed herself to go faster.

A figure emerged from the glow and her heart sang as the features became clear.

"Ranald," she said as she barreled into his arms. "It's Manus Macaidie. He killed Elspeth. Now he's coming for me."

He shoved her behind him, calling to William who was silhouetted for a moment in the torch light. "Take care of her. I'll handle Macaidie."

Ailis felt William's hand as he pulled her into the shadows. "Come," he whispered. "I'll take you to the tower."

"Nay." She shook her head, pulling free, anger and love blending together to make her strong. "I'll no' leave him. Not now. Not ever. He is my heart. If he dies, then so do I. Give me your knife."

William balked for a moment, looking ahead as Ranald moved forward, claymore held aloft. Then with a slight shrug he pulled his dirk and handed it to her, lifting his own sword. "We can follow, but you must stop when I tell you."

Ailis turned, gripping the knife, set on arguing.

"He canna fight if he thinks you're in direct danger," William said.

With a sigh of frustration Ailis accepted his words, nodding in agreement. They moved after Ranald, stopping when Manus' figure broke from the darkness. For a moment, the two men simply glared at one another, each crouching, circling in a fighter's stance. And then with a banshee's cry Manus surged forward, swinging his claymore.

Ranald lifted his in defense, the tunnel echoing with the sound of their blades clanging together. Frightened, Ailis took an involuntary step forward, lifting her knife, but William stayed her with a firm shake of his head.

The torchlight flickered as the two men fought, rocks tumbling from the walls and ceiling as they continued to swipe and parry. For moments it seemed no one was winning. Each man took blows, and Ailis felt her heart twisting with each movement they made.

Then Ranald leapt into the air, his feet pushing off of the tunnel wall as he twirled and swung his weapon, the blade cutting into Manus' upper chest, throwing him back against the wall. Hitting the ground, Ranald rounded on him again, sweeping his sword in a cutting arc that left Manus staggering and then falling to the ground.

For an instant no one moved and then Ranald turned, frowning when he saw them both standing there. But Ailis had no care. She ran to him, ignoring the fallen warrior at her feet. "Are you injured?" She ran her hands down his arms as she searched his face. "Did he hurt you?"

"Nay, lass. Only some scratches. I'm fine." He pulled back, his gaze devouring her. "And you. Did he hurt you?"

"No. I'm fine. I just…I just…" She trailed off, tears filling her eyes.

"'Tis all right, *mo ghrádh*. He canna hurt you now."

"He's dead?" she asked.

"Aye. On his way to see the devil, I'll wager." His kiss was quick and hard, full of passion and possession, and then he frowned as he pushed her back to capture her gaze. "I thought I told you to stay back." He pulled her close again, so close that she could hear his heart beat. "William?"

William stepped forward, his face red but his expression resolute. "She would no' go. Insisted she stay with you. To my mind, 'tis a fine lass who stands with her man. How could I argue?"

"How could you indeed." Ranald laughed.

"As usual I see you had all the fun without us, little brother," Benneit said as he and Kendric stepped into the light, sheathing their claymores.

Frowning, he turned to his brothers, still holding Ailis in his arms. "Shouldn't you be watching out for Macadie's men? I dinna think they'll attack us now, but there's no way to be certain."

"In truth, there is," Kendrick said. "Iain arrived with enough of his men to scuttle Macaidie's. They've headed for the hills. And with Macaidie dead," he nodded toward the body, "I'm guessing there won't be any reason for them to return."

"Iain's here?" Ranald said, his fingers stroking Ailis' nape as she snuggled closer, his heat comforting her in a way nothing else could.

"Aye, and Duncan as well. Seems the whole of Clan Chattan has come to the rescue."

"But he'll want..."Ailis paused, looking up into Ranald's eyes. "He'll want to know about us. I can tell him this was all my fault." She swallowed, suddenly afraid of his answer.

"Ach, *leannan*, there's nothing to tell. We're wed good and truly now. And no man—no' even the laird himself is going to tell me different. We'll meet him face to face and explain the situation." He brushed a kiss against her hair. "William, see to the body will you?"

The younger man hurried forward, as they moved toward Benneit and Kendric.

"I still say you have all the fun," Benneit groused.

Ailis wasn't sure if he was referencing the fight or herself, but for the moment she didn't care.

"After you talk with Duncan and Iain, I'm thinking it'll be time for a celebration," Kendric said.

The four of them headed for the entrance of the cellar. "'Tis an excellent idea, brother o' mine," Ranald said, pulling Ailis close. "But the two of you are definitely no' invited."

❧

"*I* canna leave the two of you on your own for a moment. First a handfasting and then an attempted kidnapping." Iain strode across the great hall to embrace both Ranald and Ailis.

"Well, you and Katherine set a high bar." Ranald smiled at his friend, keeping an arm around his wife.

"I'm delighted to see that neither of you is the worse for the wear. I'd thought you might have need for me, but it appears you both had things well in hand."

Ailis shivered. "We almost didn't."

"But we're fine now. What of Macaidie's men?" Ranald queried.

"Scattered. I've sent Fergus along with some of Duncan's and my men to make sure they've truly dispersed. And if not, to make sure they ken what will happen should they act against either of you again."

"And Duncan just happened to be in the area?" Ranald frowned.

"Nay. Duncan came to Duncreag when he received the news of the attack on Ailis." He gestured to the Laird who was in deep conversation with Benneit and Kendric. "And then your messenger arrived and we feared Manus would cause trouble. Which proved to be the case."

"Does Duncan know the truth about our marriage?" Ailis asked, clearly still worrying about the handfasting. Ranald promised himself he'd convince her later tonight that their union was what he wanted. And surprisingly, he realized it was true. He'd fallen in love with his wee brave wife.

"Nay, I dinna see the point in telling that part of the tale." Iain stepped back and smiled at them both. "Katherine sends her best. She wanted to come, but at the moment she canna ride."

"I'm sorry we pulled you away from home," Ailis said. "I've managed to cause everyone a lot of trouble."

"Nonsense, you became part of our family when you helped Katherine and me against your brother. And now, you're my cousin. Although I canna say much for your choice in men." His laughter filled the room and Ailis's cheeks flushed red.

"So how about a kiss from the blushing bride?" Duncan boomed as he joined them on the great hall's dais.

Bea and her husband arrived with pitchers of ale, and they all sat down at the large table. Iain and Duncan across from Ranald and Ailis, his brothers flanking the two of them in a show of solidarity.

Duncan's expression sobered. "I swear to you, lass, I dinna issue any decree ordering your marriage. Although 'tis true that Macaidie petitioned for your hand."

Ailis lifted her chin in defiance, the move one Ranald was coming to recognize. He reached over to cover her hand with his own.

"I'd ne'er agree to something like that without talking to you first. I know we argued about your taking a husband," Duncan said, "but I only ever wanted what is best for you."

"I canna say that leaving her to come home on her own was the best of plans," Bea harrumphed.

"In hindsight, perhaps no'. But I came as soon as I heard trouble was afoot."

"I appreciate all of that," Ailis said. "But now what I want is to go home, and to know that once there my clan will be safe from further attacks by Manus's men."

"Iain and I will accompany you both to Tur nan Clach. Along with our men. A show of force and support. You are part of Clan Chattan, after all. And I support your leadership of your people."

She tilted her head to look at Ranald.

"Dinna fash yourself, *mo ghrádh*, I'll be there to support you in every way." Her smile lit every corner of his heart, and he wondered what he'd done to deserve her.

"Well, I say we drink a toast to Ailis and Ranald." Benneit lifted his ale and the others at the table followed suit.

"And now, before you gentlemen start refilling those tankards," Bea said, "I think it best if Ailis comes with me. She's been through an ordeal after all."

"I'm fine," Ailis protested. "Just a bit tired and stiff." She lifted her arm to reach for her ale and Ranald snagged her wrist gently, turning it to the candlelight. The entire wrist was purple and swollen.

"God's teeth." Ranald felt anger rising. "Did Macaidie do this?"

"Nay. 'Twas Elspeth. She had a knife and tried to kill me. Manus actually saved me when he attacked her with his claymore." She shuddered.

"Elspeth?" Iain asked.

"The maidservant who kidnapped Ailis," Ranald said.

Duncan sat back and crossed his arms. "Which begs the question of how and why."

"She fancied herself in love with Manus," Ailis explained, repeating what she'd heard in the meadow. "'Twas clear that he was using her to get to me. He'd already goaded her into helping him try to have me killed."

"So Manus was behind the attack at the abbey?" Kendric asked.

"Aye. With Elspeth's help. She tricked my cousin into telling her my whereabouts. And then gave Manus' men the information."

"And when they failed," Ranald said, "he switched tactics. Tried to force you to marry him. But how did this Elspeth wind up here?"

"Holy Mother Mary, I'm afraid that one is on me," Bea said, her expression at once horrified and apologetic. "The woman came to me a few days ago, offering herself as maid of all work. She claimed to know your aunt, Ailis. Said she'd heard I needed help. Since I was indeed shorthanded, I thought nothing of it."

"Dinna fash yourself," Duncan said. "She clearly was well versed in what she was to do."

"That explains why Manus didn't ride with us. He must have gone to her." Ranald reached again for Ailis' hand. "Bea is right, *mo ghrádh*, you need to rest."

"I've ordered a bath. The hot water will do you a world of good." Bea pushed to her feet. "You're practically asleep now. Come."

Ailis turned to Ranald, lifting her brows in question. "Go," he said. "I'll be right behind you. I just need to discuss a few things with Duncan."

The men all stood as Ailis rose. Then with a small smile, she followed Bea from the room.

"You're a lucky man," Benneit said.

"Don't I know it, *bràthair*. Don't I know it."

CHAPTER 11

"*A*ch, let me see those bruises, lass."

Ailis held out her wrist for Bealag's inspection. The skin was less swollen, but angry streaks of red still interspersed with purple to mark the place where Elspeth had held her.

"This salve will put things right in no time. My sister is the best when it comes to taking care of what ails you."

"I'd put Katherine up against her any day," Ailis replied, closing her eyes as Bea rubbed the ointment into her skin.

"Iain's wife? I've no' met her, but to hear the boys tell it she hung the moon."

"She's most definitely special." Ailis smiled and opened her eyes. "But more importantly, she loves Iain. I think that's what Ranald and his brothers respect the most. 'Tis no' easy to find love. And she and Iain have not only found it, they've fought for it. Survived, and I suspect would have died for it, if need be."

"'Tis a rare thing, this kind of love," Bea said.

"You have it with Effric. I've seen the two of you together."

"Aye, that I do," she said, tying a bandage firmly in place. "And so do you with Ranald."

"Nay. We dinna have that kind of connection. I canna believe that he loves me at all, if I'm honest." She waved a hand as Bea started to interrupt her. "Oh, I know he cares. But no' like that. No' like Iain. No' with his whole heart and soul."

"I think you're wrong, child. I've known Ranald since he was no bigger than a clump o' gorse. And I've ne'er seen him as happy as when he's with you."

"But I…I…"

"You captured his heart, lass. Nothing more or less. Men have trouble expressing their feelings. They hide them beneath all that posturing and blustering. But that doesn't mean they dinna care."

"Mayhap," Ailis protested, wishing that Bea's words were true, "but there are things you don't know."

"Sweeting, whatever it is I trust my eyes. I may be old, but I'm no' blind. Ranald Macqueen loves you. 'Tis as plain as the nose on yer face." Bea smiled, and smoothed back Ailis hair. "You just have to believe and take a leap of faith."

"If only it were that easy. But if I've learned nothing else in this life, it's that men canna be trusted. Just look at what my father did to my mother. And what my brother did to me."

"Ach lass, I know it hasn't been an easy life. But things are different now. Col and Alisdair are gone. Your mother, God rest her soul, would want you to move on. "

"She'd want me to take care of my people—*her* people."

"Aye, she would. But not at the expense of your happiness. That would be her first wish. That you find peace and love."

"How can you know that?" Ailis asked, wishing there were some magic that would make her see her future the way that Bea did. That would allow her to hope—to believe.

"Because I knew yer mother, lass. When we were both young we were inseparable. And then later, after she married Col, 'twas more difficult to see each other, but we ne'er lost touch completely."

"You were at Tur nan Clach?"

"Nay, Col would no' allow it. But your Auntie Elizabet arranged for us to meet at her cottage. 'Twas just after you were born."

"I don't remember." Ailis shook her head, tears filling her eyes.

"You'd no' recollect. You were just a wee bairn. But, oh, she loved you so. You were the light of her life."

Ailis reached for Bea's hands. "What was she like?"

"She looked much as you do. Her hair was long and fair like yours. Her eyes the clear blue of a loch in winter. And when she smiled everyone else smiled, too."

"I wish I remembered more."

"You do." Bea smiled, and touched her fingers to her breast. "In here, in your heart. And you can honor your mother by living your life. By loving the people at Tur nan Clach and by loving Ranald."

"But…"

Bea lifted a finger to Ailis' lips. "Nay lass, there is no but… only the two of you. Together you're better. Stronger. You simply have to believe. Trust in Ranald. It's what your mother would tell you if she were here."

Bea wrapped Ailis in an embrace she felt to her core, and suddenly she felt as if anything was possible. And then the older woman stepped away. "I have something for you." She reached into a pocket sewn into the waist of her apron. "It was your mother's. She gave it to me the day I met you."

Ailis stared at the silver clan badge in Bea's hand. The rampant lion with sword in paw, *misneach*, courage, carved into the swirling silver, a ragged notch in the edge the only thing marring its beauty. "'Tis beautiful," she whispered, as if the badge would suddenly startle and take flight.

"Aye. The badge belongs to the Comyns. You're a Comyn on your mother's side. This belonged to her granny. And it seems to me that it should belong to you."

Ailis took the brooch, her fingers closing around it, recognizing the warmth, her mind turning from thoughts of her mother, to Quinn and the abbey.

"Thank you." Ailis smiled up at the older woman, her heart singing with hope. "You can't possibly know what this means to me."

"'Tis enough to see that I've made you happy. 'Tis what your mother would have wanted." Bea reached for the ointment and bandages just as Ranald strode into the chamber. With a hug for each of them Bea waltzed through the door, leaving the two of them staring at each other. Ailis carefully placed the brooch on the table. There'd be time enough to tell Ranald what it meant later.

This moment—now—was for the two of them. It was time to take that leap of faith.

～

*A*ilis opened her mouth to say something but Ranald didn't give her the chance, instead, crossing the room to pull her close, his lips finding hers, the touch sending heat sparking through him. He traced the line of her shoulders, reveling in the silky feel of her skin beneath his fingers. Then his hand slid lower, finding her breast beneath the soft linen of her night rail. She moaned, the sound sending all rational thought scattering away.

His thumb rasped against her nipple, the little nub tightening as he deepened their kiss, breathing in her essence even as he caressed her body. His lips moved across her skin, down the hollow of her cheek until he reached her ear, feeling her shiver beneath his touch.

He dropped his head lower, her hands twining in his hair as he trailed kisses along the line of her shoulder, his hands continuing to move across her skin. She tasted sweet and salty and he inhaled her fragrance, his body hardening as his mouth found the crest of her breast.

Urgency built within him. The need for something more. Something beyond the physical. Connection, belonging. A desire to become one. The physical pull was strong. But there was something more. Something magnificent. Something worth fighting for.

With desire shimmering between them she pushed closer, grinding her hips against his. It was Ranald's turn to groan as she fumbled with the brooch holding his plaid. When the pin opened the soft wool dropped to the floor, and together they pulled the rest of their clothes free.

Skin to skin he pushed her backwards, falling onto the bed, careful to keep from crushing her beneath him. He lifted his head to gaze into her eyes, his heart pounding, his body hard and ready. "I want you, lass. Right here. Right now. So please tell me if you're no' ready."

"I want you, Ranald Macqueen," she whispered, her gaze still locked with his. "Now and forever. If you'll have me."

"God's blood, I swear you'll be the death of me, *leannan*. I've never wanted a woman more."

"Then take me, Ranald. Take me now."

With a swiftness that threatened to rob them both of breath he thrust home, the contact of her breasts against his chest beyond exquisite. He took her lips and drank deeply, wanting nothing more in this moment than this woman. Their fervor increased, each touch, each movement raising the stakes, heightening the pleasure.

His hands settled beneath her hips, lifting her until her

legs circled him, their gazes still locked. He pulled out and then slid deep, holding her in place as the pure pleasure of the movement threatened to shatter them both.

They began to move in earnest then. In and out, in and out. Each stroke taking them higher, until he could no longer tell where he ceased and she began.

He closed his eyes, letting sensation take control. Aware of only the feel of her heat surrounding him, caressing him, binding them together with every stroke. Their bodies locked together they moved faster and faster, until the pleasure exploded into an inferno of heat and light, Ranald's body and mind oblivious of everything except the power of his passion and the feel of her breath against his skin.

~

*A*ilis lay in the bed and watched the moonlight as it danced across the room, bits of dust glimmering in the reflected silver. Ranald lay with one leg slung over her thigh, the gesture comforting in a way that made her feel safe and protected. She snuggled closer, his heart beating beneath her ear, his scent filling her with contentment and joy.

"Is it always like this between a man and a woman?" she asked. "This powerful, I mean?"

"Nay, *mo ghrádh.* What we have is special. Beyond what most men and women experience when they're together."

"And you're sure you want to stay? I mean beyond just the honor of a promise?" She hated that she sounded so insecure, but Bea was right. She had to take the risk. She had to bare herself so that he knew.

"I want nothing more. But the same goes for you. You have to want me in the way that I want you."

"And that is?" she questioned, moving closer still.

"I love you, *leannan*. With the breadth and depth of my being. I love you."

She smiled, her heart leaping with pure joy. "And I love you. So much so that I'll go with you to Stirling—and wait for you there while you fight for our king."

"I appreciate the offer. You canna know how much it means. But I've talked to Duncan, and he understands that I'm needed at Tur nan Clach. He's going to convince the king to let Kendric take my place. I'll stand with you as you claim the lairdship, and together we'll lead the clan. *Our* clan."

"Together. I like the sound of that." She laced her fingers with his. "Mayhap, Manus did us both a favor."

"Or perhaps 'twas simply destiny that we found each other again. Either way, you're mine now, Ailis Davidson."

"And you are mine." She smiled up at him as the little brooch winked in the moonlight.

"We'll head to Tur nan Clach on the morrow."

"Aye," she concurred, rubbing her cheek against his chest. "But first, there's one last thing I need to do."

~

The morning mist still swirled along the ground as they rode up to the abbey. Iain, Kendric and Benneit had insisted on accompanying them while the rest of the company prepared to leave for Tur nan Clach upon their return.

The winter wind whistled through the trees, the gray clouds matching the solemnity of Ailis' mood. Ranald dismounted and tied his horse to a low hanging branch, then reached up to encircle her waist, lifting her to the ground. At his signal, the others waited on their horses as the two of them walked into the shadows of the abbey.

Cuimeanach was much as she'd left it. The ceiling still open to the skies, the altar broken and empty, the archway leading to the crypt illuminated by the weak morning sun. Reaching for Ranald's hand, they walked together to the foot of the two crypts adorned with the knight and his lady. Their faces were blank—peaceful. A promise that eternity was without strife or worry.

She reached out a hand and smoothed her fingers across the lady's face. "They saved me, you know. The two of them and Quinn."

"Then I owe them all a debt I can never repay." He wrapped an arm around her shoulders as she shrugged in response.

"Who can say what will happen in the future. We know that nothing is carved in stone." She smiled at the play on words and reached into her cloak, producing the silver clan badge. "Clan Comyn," she whispered. "'Tis fitting, is it not?"

"Aye, that it is. But are you sure you want to leave it, lass? It belonged to your mother after all."

"She'd have wanted it this way. I believe that. Here," she touched her chest, "in my heart."

"Then let it be done," he said, dropping a kiss on her forehead and then stepping away, leaving her alone with the graves.

"I dinna know if you can hear me, Quinn, but I need you to know that I'm all right. And that your saving me has led to the possibility of a future I'd never dared dream. So thank you. And Godspeed."

She leaned down and nestled the brooch into a small crevice at the lady's feet, then with a sigh turned back to Ranald, holding out her hand.

He took it, linking his fingers with hers, pulling her close. "It's time to go home, *mo ghràdh.*"

They walked back out into the soft winter sunlight towards Kendric, Iain, and Benneit. While behind them, in the tiny chapel, the clan badge began to glow. Then, with a final flash of silver, it disappeared. The knight and his lady were alone.

Read on for an excerpt of Dee Davis' Cottage in the Mist!

Scotland, 1468

THERE WAS DANGER. Bram could feel it all around him. Fire raced up the wooden steps that lead up to the door leading into the tower. And he could see more flames thrusting out of the windows, black smoke spiraling into the night sky. Throwing his plaid over his face, he ran up the steps, but was stopped by one of the tower's guards.

The man raised his claymore, his eyes narrowed as the deadly blade began its descent. Bram pivoted, and then swung his own weapon, confused as to where he was and why he was fighting. The man fell, only to be replaced by another. Bram called to him, some part of him recognizing a face that still seemed a stranger, but this man, too, seemed intent only on stopping him.

His mind argued that nothing made sense, even as his heart screamed that he must get inside. If he did not then that which was most precious to him would be lost. He knew this as surely as he drew breath.

With a twist and a parry he drew the man off, and then made quick work of him, dashing through the opening of the tower, down the hallway and into the great hall. A place meant for comfort it offered only danger now. It too was full of flame, and lined with enemies.

Again the thought brought him up short. But there was no time to try and understand. Fear pushed him forward. He surged into the fray, moving toward the stairway at the far end of the room. It gave access to the chambers above and it was there he knew he would find her.

His brain recoiled. Find who? But his heart urged him forward, and he fought his way to the bottom of the steps, then ran up them, taking them two at a time, knowing the other swordsmen were fast on his heels.

At the top he froze for a moment, the thick smoke disorienting him. The fire was much worse here. Pushing forward, he breathed through the heavy wool of his plaid, keeping sword at the ready. The first chamber was empty. As was the solar and the chamber beyond it. But then from down the narrow hallway he heard a cry.

Heart thundering in his ears, he ran through the flames and smoke. A timber fell, glancing off of his shoulder, and he hardly felt it, the need to find her overriding everything else.

He called for her, his voice swallowed by the raging fire. Another timber fell, and a wall collapsed. He jumped across a gaping hole in the floor, landing hard, but still moving. The doorway ahead was edged in flames, the smoke and fire roiling like some kind of evil spirit.

Ignoring the danger, he sprinted forward, through the opening, again calling her name.

And then, through the shimmering heat, he saw her, tied

to the bedframe, her long hair unbound, her green eyes wide with fear.

"Go back," she screamed.

But he pushed onward, stumbling as still more of the burning tower fell. "I'll no' leave you." His words were whipped away by the inferno surrounding them. But he knew that she had heard him.

There were only a few feet between them now. There was bruising on her face, and a trickle of blood at the corner of her beautiful mouth, and he swore there would be hell to pay.

But first, he had to free her.

He reached out a hand, but as he did so, the ceiling above him crashed to the ground. One moment he was looking into her eyes—and the next, she was gone.

Double Danger

Dire Distraction

Matchmaker Chronicles

A Match Made on Madison

Set Up In SoHo

Time After Time Series

Everything In Its Time

Winter's Kiss

Cottage in the Mist

The Promise

Wild Highland Rose

Triad Series

Fade to Gray

Devil May Care Series

Hell Fire (novella)

Hell's Fury (novella)

ABOUT THE AUTHOR

Bestselling author **Dee Davis** worked in association management before turning her hand to writing. Her highly acclaimed first novel, *Everything In Its Time*, was published in July 2000. Since then, among others, she's won the Booksellers Best, Golden Leaf, Texas Gold and Prism awards, and been nominated for the National Readers Choice Award, the Holt and three RT Reviewers Choice Awards. To date, she is the author of over thirty books and novellas. When not sitting at the computer, Dee spends time in her 1802 farmhouse with her husband and cardigan welsh corgis.

Visit Dee at http://www.deedavis.com or catch up with her on Facebook at http://www.facebook.com/deedavisbooks or follow her on Twitter at http://twitter.com/deesdavis
   Photo: Marti Corn

Made in the USA
Coppell, TX
18 September 2022

83292625R00075